THE HAMMER OF DR VALENTINE

A SNOWBOOKS HORROR NOVELLA

Proudly published by Snowbooks

Snowbooks Ltd.
email: info@snowbooks.com
www.snowbooks.com.

British Library Cataloguing in Publication Data.
A catalogue record for this book is available
from the British Library.

Paperback: 978-1-911390-93-0
Ebook: 978-1-911390-92-3

To Simon + Cate

"My revenge has spread over
centuries - + has just begun!"
With much love + admiration,

John Llewellyn Probert -

THE HAMMER OF
DR VALENTINE

JOHN LLEWELLYN PROBERT

The Hammer of Dr Valentine is respectfully dedicated to all those highly talented and skilled men and women who helped make the productions of Hammer Films such fabulous entertainments.

And especially, Peter Cushing and Christopher Lee.

Because, gentlemen, you really were the best.

ACKNOWLEDGEMENTS

This time, my thanks have to go first of all to everyone who bought The Nine Deaths of Dr Valentine. You're the reason this second book has seen print, everyone, so if you enjoyed this one too give yourselves a big pat on the back for being so supportive of this little indulgence of mine. I had at least as much fun writing it as I did the first, so thank you very much indeed.

Simon Marshall-Jones of Spectral Press will always deserve my eternal gratitude for giving me the opportunity to write the first one, and this sequel.

This book would not exist if Hammer Films had not existed. Indeed, I probably wouldn't be the person I am now if Hammer Films had not gone down the route of producing elegant, gory, sexy, well—acted gothics from the late 1950s. I'm not going to thank specific individuals, partly because the films Hammer made always felt like a group effort to me, but mainly because I would hate to miss anyone important out.

The story you have just read would not exist without Hammer Films. The book you are holding would not exist without the efforts of my publishers. I, on the other hand, would not exist without Mrs Kathleen Probert (aka the horror writer Thana Niveau). And so this last thank you is for her. Once again, she has had to sit and listen to me reading out the entire text of The Hammer of Dr Valentine. Her support and companionship is, and always had been, priceless. Thank you, my love I know you enjoy all this stuff just as much as I do, and that in itself has a value beyond measure.

THE HAMMER OF DR. VALENTINE

ONE

The man's body flew into the air.

It is not easy to fling a sixteen stone man from a cliff top into a Welsh valley, and the considerable velocity necessary to perform this feat had been attained by the use of the catapult into which the man had been secured. The device had been fashioned from heavy oak, and its spring—loaded mechanism employed the very finest high tensile British steel, just to ensure there were no mistakes.

No-one saw the body land in the valley below.

This was intentional, which is why this complex and dangerous procedure was being performed at night. Behind the stark outline of the catapult, itself only partly concealed by the surrounding foliage, the towers of Castell Coch stood impassive, their silhouettes black against the deepest blue of the night sky.

Prior to his release into the air, four guide ropes of woven steel had been run through the man's clothes. These extended from the catapult to the ground below. It was intended that the flying, and very much still-living, victim land in a very specific place, namely onto the point of the heavy gold cross that had been obtained with some difficulty from a local cathedral, and set into the ground of the valley below at a precise angle.

Following that had come the moment of truth.

The lever was depressed, the spring mechanism released, and

the sometimes-screaming, sometimes-pleading projectile was launched into the chill of the Welsh night.

The landing was perfect.

Even from a distance it was possible to see, with the aid of a pair of opera glasses, that the uppermost point of the cross had pierced its intended victim between the shoulder blades, or scapulae, as the perpetrator of this ghastly crime much preferred to call them. The blood-smeared tip emerged from the man's chest, and he hung there for a moment, gurgling amidst the gore, before his legs stopped twitching, and all was still.

The man responsible for this was the same man who had supervised the removal of the cross from St David's Cathedral while posing as a high-ranking member of the clergy. He had also arranged for the design and construction of the catapult in Zurich, and its subsequent transportation to the UK under more secrecy than even MI5 was capable of. The man who had calculated the angle of trajectory, the arc of velocity and, most important, the speed at which a sixteen stone man needed to be travelling in order for the enormous crucifix to run him through, looked over the cliff's edge. He nodded with satisfaction to the beautiful girl beside him, the one who had lured the unsuspecting victim to this isolated spot, clad in the pink chiffon dress she was still wearing. The scene in the valley below looked very similar to the one from the film that had inspired it, right down to the black cape with the red satin lining that the victim had been forced to wear before being placed in the catapult.

Yes, he thought. That should get their attention.

That should get their attention very nicely.

TWO

"An Evening of Ancient Egyptian Splendour and Excitement!"

Margaret Upchurch, Mags to her (admittedly very few) friends, looked at the elaborate lettering on the gilt-edged invitation card for a third time, and wondered if she was doing the right thing. On the maroon velveteen quilt of her hotel room's double bed lay the elaborate costume that had accompanied both the invitation card and the details of the booking that had been made for her for that evening. Fancy dress really wasn't her thing, but if Professor Fuchs, whoever he was, wanted to hold a press conference at the British Museum to herald the return of his latest expedition, and have everyone attending dressed up in period costume to satisfy some peculiar kink of his, who was she to argue?

Mags grinned to herself. Oh yes, she was definitely going, if only to prove a point to those bastards who ran the British Museum, the ones who had tried to ban her from the place after that story she had written detailing their use of unpaid illegal immigrants as cleaners. It had all proved to be unfounded, of course, but the paper hadn't minded that — her story had helped to pick up a slow news day. Besides, it had been her first turn for that particular rag since all the business with that lunatic doctor a couple of years back. And, she thought to herself, with any luck there'd be at least a few pieces of juicy gossip at the post-conference party that should allow her to put together something the public would lap up, if only about how their money was going to waste on ridiculous endeavours like this one. Of course she had no idea if the expedition had been funded with public money, and in all likelihood it probably hadn't, but she saw no reason why she shouldn't hint at it in her article.

She held up the dress that had been sent to her. The size was perfect, and she nodded with approval. Someone had evidently done their homework. It was a bit revealing, though. Too much midriff and a fair old bit of cleavage would be on show, but at thirty one Mags prided herself on her looks having very much helped to get her to where she was today, and with any luck it would help loosen the tongues of any men who would be too busy staring at her tits to realise they'd dropped themselves in it, quote-wise.

At least the skirt was floor-length, she thought as she tugged it on. The shoes didn't seem exactly period, though — surely the ancient Egyptians didn't go in for strappy gold buckles and high heels? Not that she minded — they were a damned sight more elegant than whatever flat-soled sandal-things people probably wore back then. She slipped them on, again noting that they were a perfect fit. Whoever had organised this really had taken care of everything.

The phone in her room rang and she answered it, spoke four words and replaced the receiver.

Right down to the taxi to take her there, she thought, with approval.

*

The female taxi driver was just a little younger than she was. Why Mags found this vaguely disconcerting she couldn't say, but it was most likely because she suddenly felt very odd sitting in a car being driven by a normally-dressed attractive young girl while Mags felt as if she was on the way to a do for drag queens.

"It's a fancy dress party," she felt moved to explain. She clutched at the bejewelled headdress she had found it necessary to take off so she could get into the car, and awaited the driver's reply.

The girl said nothing, but Mags was sure her brown eyes held a knowing glint as she checked out Mags' reflection in her rear-view mirror.

Mags shut up after that.

London is always busy, but the traffic that Tuesday evening was especially bad. It was well past the time she was meant to get there when Mags was eventually deposited on the pavement outside what she assumed must be the British Museum. She showed her disdain to the driver by neglecting to give a tip, and it was only once the girl had driven away that she realised she wasn't in front of the building's main entrance in Great Russell Street at all, but some godforsaken side road round the back.

She was about to start walking when a nearby door opened.

The man standing in the doorway was in silhouette but he appeared to be wearing the uniform of a British Museum security guard, and that was good enough for her.

"Can you help me, please?" she said, fluttering her eyelashes but keeping her voice firm. For some reason most of the men she knew seemed to prefer it when her voice had a harder edge. She held out the invitation. "I'm supposed to be at this. I know I'm late but the bloody cab driver decided to take the long way round."

The man stepped into the light and now she could see that he was a little older than she had first thought. His hair was concealed beneath the black cap, of course, but the streaks of grey in his sideburns lent him an edge of sophistication that was only augmented by his voice when he spoke.

"Ah yes," he said, once he had read the proffered card, "yes of course. Do come in. You are expected."

Mags followed him through the doorway, wondering how such a well-spoken man might have ended up in such a dead end job.

Perhaps there was even a story in it.

"Have you been working here long?" she asked as she followed him down what looked like a service corridor, if the walls of whitewashed breeze-block and intermittent dull fluorescent strip lighting were anything to go by.

"Not long," came the reply from in front of her. The man didn't turn round. "But these days you have to take jobs where you find them, don't you agree?"

"I suppose so." Mags didn't really care. Her feet were starting to hurt and she needed a drink. "So what did you do — before this, I mean?"

"I've been out of work for a couple of years," he said as they took a left turn, "but I've managed to find ways of occupying myself. Nevertheless, I'm sure you can appreciate how relieved I am to be here this evening."

"But you had a job before that?" Mags was nothing if not persistent. After all, she had made a career from it.

"Oh yes," said the man with the lovely voice, "but unfortunately it was all taken away from me."

"How?" Mags knew she was getting ahead of herself but if it turned out to be interesting she could always ask him to go back over anything juicy.

The man paused, and turned around, allowing her to see the sadness in his eyes. "An accident," he said. "A death."

"Of a loved one, that much is obvious," said Mags, hoping she was sounding more sympathetic to his ears than to hers. "Was it someone close?"

The man had moved off again now, and she had to struggle to keep up with him. "My daughter," he said as they came out of the grim little tunnel and into what looked like the museum proper. Colourful murals depicting life in ancient Egypt adorned the walls, while at regular intervals glass cases on plinths housed tiny artefacts that looked like ragged pieces of junk shop tat but which were probably priceless.

"That's awful," said Mags in her 'sympathy at the loss of a child' voice she had honed to perfection when she was working on a kidnapping story a few years ago. "What happened?" Before she could stop herself she added, "Was it medical malpractice?" Those always made wonderful sob stories.

Again the man paused, his face this time still turned away from her. "It's not really any of your business," he said, "but as a matter of fact, yes. It was a medical misdemeanour that led to her demise."

Mags thanked whoever or whatever it was that had caused her to be late. If she played her cards right she might be able to bag herself a thousand words of copy without having to go to this stupid Egyptian thing at all.

"That's terrible," she said, as they passed a man-sized statue of Anubis that had seen better days. This time she made sure to add a little quaver to her sympathetic tone. "But doctors can be real sons of bitches sometimes — arrogant, conceited, completely full of themselves. They think they're God when in fact they have absolutely no idea what they're doing."

The man stopped again and turned to face her. Ahead Mags could hear music, laughter, the tinkle of glasses. She hoped she would be able to get everything she wanted out of this bloke before they reached the party.

"I had no idea you were a member of the medical profession," he said.

Mags laughed like a harpy at that, forgetting for an instant what had happened to the man she was talking to. "I'm not a doctor!" she said.

"In that case you must forgive me," The man turned away and started walking again, towards the sounds of merrymaking. "For a moment I was under the mistaken impression that you knew what you were talking about."

Mags frowned. Whoever he might have been in the past, this jumped-up bloody security guard had no right to talk to her like that!

"Just a minute," she said, chasing after him. "I'll have you know that I'm a journalist, and a couple of years ago I covered a story for one of the national dailies about quite possibly the most insane member of 'the medical profession' this country has ever seen!"

Her outburst seemed to have little effect on her companion. "We have arrived at your destination, Miss Upchurch," the security guard said, opening a white side door between two mummy cases. He indicated she should step inside. Before she did so he added, "Please accept my apologies for any remarks I may have made that might have upset you. I do hope that what I have just said doesn't spoil your evening, and that you don't leave tonight feeling too crushed."

Mags paid little attention. She had heard that kind of thing before too many times for it to have any effect on her. The laughter and chatting was very loud now, almost abnormally so, and she pointedly ignored the security guard as she stepped into the room.

The large, white, empty room.

At first Mags thought that the chamber in which she found herself had to be a vestibule, a conduit to the party proper. But the solid walls on every side of her told her that was not so.

She took two steps forward, and switched off the reel-to-reel tape recorder that was playing on the small square table in front of her.

Any noise that suggested a party might be taking place ceased. Now, all Mags could hear was the sounds of her own rapid breathing, and the click of her heels on the white tiled floor as she took another step forward.

The room wasn't quite empty.

There was something on the far wall. Lots of things, in fact. Some were in black and white, others were in colour. Some were pasted onto the wall, others held in place with drawing pins.

Newspaper headlines, magazine covers, columns and clippings, all meticulously cut out and pieced together.

All about the same thing.

Mags recognised her contribution to the makeshift mural, but it would have been difficult not to. Placed centrally, and outlined in bright red marker pen, was a piece entitled "Doctor Death — The Mad Medic Who Slew His Own Kind".

She was reaching out to touch the print when there was a voice from behind her.

"I was never Doctor Death, you know."

Mags turned. The security officer was standing in the doorway, but now he looked very different. The cap was gone, and his uniform had been substituted for an expensive-looking dinner suit. The black cloak with its red satin lining was the crowning extravagance, yet somehow it didn't look out of place on him.

The man radiated authority, and for the first time in many years Mags felt intimidated. She could feel her heart pounding as she did her best to stammer some kind of a reply.

"W — w — weren't you?" she said.

The man tutted. "Goodness me, no. If you had done your research properly you would have known that." He held out his arms and flicked his wrists with a flourish, causing the cloak to fall back over his shoulders. "Vincent Price played, rather indirectly, a character called Doctor Death in the 1974 film *Madhouse*. As I just said, if you had done your research properly for that…story that is pinned up there, you would have known that. Just as you would have known that *Madhouse*, a film considerably inferior to his wonderful *Theatre of Blood*, was not one of the inspirations I drew on to exact my revenge."

Mags was filled with a mixture of dread and excitement as she realised who she was talking to. She had hoped to get a good story tonight but she had never dreamed she might be getting such an exclusive.

She drew herself up to her most statuesque, pleased she had put the headdress on when she had exited the taxi as it gave her extra height. She pushed out her quite respectable bosom, and imagined that she really was a queen of Egypt, just to give herself a bit of extra confidence. "You're Dr Edward Valentine," she said.

It was a statement, not a question. The man in the doorway nodded in response as he looked her up and down.

"I have to admit I did a splendid job estimating your measurements for that costume," Dr Valentine said. "It's such a shame your written work was never as presentable as you."

"If my story was that bad, tell me where I went wrong." Mags was always ready to take advantage of a situation, and she was delighted to realise that being faced by a flamboyant psychotic serial killer hadn't dampened her ardour one bit. "Give me your own, personal side of things. The story only Dr Valentine himself could tell. That would be something I could sell to the highest bidder. And let me assure you I know people who would be willing to bid very highly indeed. We could both end up very rich."

"I suppose we could." Valentine seemed uninterested as he rubbed his palms together. "The problem with the kind of reporting you do, Miss Upchurch — it is Miss, isn't it?" Mags nodded. "Yes, I thought it would have to be. The problem with your type is that the truth is never enough. It has to be embellished, exaggerated, turned into a story to thrill and chill, to be, by turns, both worrying and reassuring, and most of all, to give the public what disreputable publications like the ones pinned on that wall there mistakenly believe the public want."

"Not mistakenly," said Mags, jerking a thumb behind her. "Do you have any idea how many copies we sold of that story of mine?"

Valentine shook his head. "I don't have any idea, Miss Upchurch, I have an exact idea. Which brings me to why you are here today."

Mags' eyes brightened. "You mean you really want me to tell your story?"

There was a long pause before Valentine gave his reply.

"Not exactly," he said eventually, before permitting himself the faintest of smiles. "What I really want, is for you to be a part of the next one."

It took a moment for that to sink in.

"What do you mean?" Now the confidence had drained from Mags' voice, to be replaced by quivering uncertainty.

"Exactly what I said," Valentine replied as he adjusted something on the inside of the door. "Now, it takes around four minutes to read that prattling barrage of nonsense you called a newspaper story, so that is how long I intend to give you to try to escape this place. I would wish you luck, but as you can probably understand, that's hardly the point. And as I mentioned beforehand, I hope this little experience won't leave you feeling too crushed."

And with that he was gone, closing the door behind him.

Mags ran after him and rattled the handle. She expected it to be locked, and so she was surprised when it turned easily and the door opened.

It also set the timer mechanism ticking that Dr Valentine had attached to the handle.

Mags looked at the counter, which now showed there were less than four minutes left until...what? Was there a bomb in here? Surely not in the British Museum? Even Valentine wouldn't be insane enough or even capable of destroying a major British landmark.

If, of course, that was in fact where she was.

Mags remembered being dropped off in that unfamiliar back street, of the long walk down those grim corridors to this room. She stepped out into the passageway. The mummy cases that flanked the doorway were still there, but now they looked less convincing than they had when she had passed them before. Now they looked more like props for a television show.

Or a film.

Oh, God.

The methods by which Valentine had taken revenge on those doctors came back to her vividly, horribly.

She looked at the costume she was wearing, at the newspaper clippings behind her, at the fake mummy cases, and wondered what he had planned.

She didn't have to wait long.

The timer was still counting down, but already the walls were starting to creak around her, the fake murals starting to crack, the fake statuary beginning to wobble. There was a rumble from above. Mags looked up and coughed as plaster dust from the gaping rent in the ceiling caught in her throat.

She ran back the way she had come, but now the door to the exit corridor had all but vanished, a white outline flush with the wall that surrounded it the only evidence there had been a door there in the first place. She looked around her, realising now that there was no other way out, and that Dr Valentine had never intended for her to escape.

She hammered on the door in rage, in fury, and finally in desperation, screaming for help even though she knew no-one could hear her, no-one who would come to her aid, anyway. Back in the room papered with clippings the timer reached zero while Mags crouched, hands over her head, waiting for the inevitable blast.

She had time to scream just once as the ceiling cracked in half. Then the roof of the building caved in and she wasn't aware of anything anymore.

THREE

When the telephone rings between two and three in the morning, it can only ever be to convey bad news.

It took some time for John Spalding to register that the jangling noise wasn't part of the dream he was having. His thoughts were still very fuzzy as he turned on his bedside lamp and picked up the receiver. On the other end of the line a voice claimed they were Detective Inspector someone-or-other, asked him to confirm his identity, and then explained that he was needed to identify a body. Now.

"I beg your pardon?" Spalding struggled out of the sheets and sat on the side of the bed. On the nightstand, just next to the brand new reissue of Lotte Eisner's *The Haunted Screen* that he had agreed to review for *The Observer*, the misty red display of the clock read 2.27am.

A body. Now. At the mortuary.

"I'm sorry, but I'm a film journalist," Spalding explained, still trying and failing to wake up. "I don't do deaths unless it's someone famous." He sat up, instantly wide awake at the sudden thought. "Is it someone famous?" he asked.

"It's someone you knew," said the voice, "and you're the only one of her close personal contacts who's answering the phone at this hour so I need you to come here now, please."

It took Spalding thirty minutes to get there. Despite its reputation as a never-sleeping metropolis, London was dead silent, and the black cab had no problem getting him across the city.

"What the bloody hell do you want to come here at this time of night for?" the driver asked him as the car pulled up to the rear of the hospital. Three police cars were already gathered there.

"Your guess is as good as mine," Spalding replied as he got out. He watched the man drive away before turning to face the gaunt concrete of the building before him.

He was greeted by a uniformed police officer, who led him through a pair of flopping plastic swing doors and down a corridor that was so poorly lit Spalding could barely see where he was going. He was ushered into a bare room where two men sat at a table littered with empty coffee cups. He presumed that the tarnished black telephone sat in the middle had been the one used to call him.

"Mr John Spalding?" A balding man, who more resembled an ageing wrestler in a mustard-coloured trenchcoat than a policeman, rose to greet him. Spalding recognised the voice. "I'm DI Derek Martinus. We spoke on the phone." He indicated the rumpled man next to him. "This is Dr Manners, he's our forensic pathologist. He'll take you to see her."

Spalding frowned. "Who?"

The DI and the pathologist exchanged glances.

"Perhaps you'd better take a seat," Martinus offered.

Spalding brushed imaginary debris from the cheap grey plastic chair before sitting down. It was as uncomfortable as it looked.

"As I said on the phone," the DI explained, "I'm sorry to have had to drag you down here, but yours was the only number on her mobile that we could get an answer from."

"She?" Spalding hardly knew any women, at least not to the degree that he'd be called down here under such circumstances.

"A friend of yours, or at the very least a colleague." Martinus' face was grim as he told Spalding the story. "At eleven o'clock this evening we received a call to come to Montague Place. It's near the British Museum, just off Russell Square. When we arrived we found something strange. Something very strange indeed."

"Well you're certainly good at building suspense, Inspector." Spalding felt a tinge of irritation. "So who exactly did you find?"

Martinus paused before coming out with his revelation. "We believe the body to be that of Margaret Upchurch," he said, "a young lady who is in the same line of work as yourself, I believe?"

15

Spalding was no longer listening. The last time he had seen Mags she had been slinking out of his bedroom, but not before telling him what a lovely time she had had, and how they must meet up again sometime.

Mags was dead?

"It's true she didn't have any surviving close family," Spalding said, his voice shaking a little now, "and to be honest I have no idea if anyone related to her lives in London."

Martinus nodded. "You understand my predicament then, sir?"

Spalding agreed. "It's been nearly two years, but I'm sure she can't have changed too much in that time. I shouldn't have any problem identifying her if that's what you need."

Martinus and the doctor exchanged glances.

"Well, there is a bit of a problem there, sir," said the policeman.

Spalding wondered why the DI was acting so shiftily. "Go on."

Martinus seemed almost embarrassed. Good God, Spalding thought, Mags hadn't bitten off more than she could chew, had she? She had always been a bit of a fan of the rough stuff but he didn't think she would ever get herself properly hurt.

"When we found her, her body was..." Martinus paused again.

Well go on! Spalding was getting impatient now. Her body was what? Dressed in kinky getup? Twisted into an obscene position? In several pieces with messages carved into the flesh?

"Her body was...covered with bandages."

Spalding let out a sigh of relief. "You mean she was found outside a hospital?"

Martinus shook his head. "No sir. I mean we found her lying in the street, covered in bandages. She'd been wrapped in them from head to toe, with just a space for the eyes. Of course by the time we found her the blood had soaked through in quite a few places. The blood from the injuries she'd sustained."

Spalding suddenly wished he smoked again. Christ, Mags. What did you get yourself into?

"What kind of injuries?"

Martinus scratched his head. "Well as far as we can tell she was inside the building we found her near when it collapsed. Forensics are going through everything now, but it looks as if the whole lot came down on top of her, crushing every bone in her body." Martinus looked to the pathologist for confirmation. He was rewarded with a brisk nod. "Then someone...someone..."

Spalding tapped the desk. "Presumably I am actually going to see her in a minute, Inspector, so you may as well just tell me."

Martinus nodded. "Thank you," he said. "I never was good at breaking news gently." He took a deep breath before continuing. "For some reason someone dragged Miss Upchurch out of the rubble, wrapped her entire body in bandages, and then left her in the street to be found. In fact for all we know the person who did it was the same one who tipped us off as well."

Spalding shrugged. "Maybe whoever wrapped her up was trying to save her?"

Martinus paused for a moment before he answered that one.

"No sir. We don't think they were trying to save her. Quite the reverse, in fact."

Spalding looked from one man to the other. "What do you mean?"

"There was a slow acting poison soaked into the bandages. As if someone wanted her to survive the accident inside the building, and then die slowly wrapped up like that. And that's not the only weird thing. They also used a very particular type of poison."

17

Martinus looked at Dr Manners, who uttered the only word to pass his lips since Spalding had arrived.

"Formaldehyde."

Martinus leaned over Spalding and placed both his hands flat on the table. It creaked as he did so.

"So that's what we have, Mr Spalding. And why, before you do us the courtesy of identifying the crushed and mutilated body of Margaret Upchurch, I have to ask you if you can think of any reason why someone would want to crush a young woman to the point where she was nearly dead, and then wrap her up in bandages soaked with embalming fluid?"

FOUR

"Is it much further?"

Michael Brennan mopped his forehead as he followed the girl down the dirt track, doing his best to keep his eyes off parts of her anatomy that a man of his age could probably go to prison for staring at, much less touching these days. Of course it would help if she wasn't wearing the kind of school uniform he could have sworn went out of fashion in the nineteen fifties, complete with straw boater, tightly buttoned blue blazer, and skirt the shortness of which he was sure he had described as 'one of the reasons our country is in the state is now' in an article of his on declining moral standards in one of the more popular tabloids.

Of course, that had been a long time ago, and he had been the author of a lot more outraged newsprint since that article about the morally bankrupt state of many of Britain's teenaged girls. That was the one that had got him in the door, though. That, and the supremely angry column he had provided about the threat to the children of both today and tomorrow as a result of the kinds of films they were allowed to watch. "If we are not careful," he remembered writing with some degree of pride, "we are creating within our midst a whole generation of Dr Valentines, who would not hesitate to recreate some of the shocking things they have seen on screen just for kicks". It had helped that he had been the one to cover the Dr Valentine affair for the paper as well, making the most of his contacts in the Bristol police force to give him the inside facts, as well as plenty of gossip and conjecture that he had been able to weave into a seamless whole to give him his first major set of headlines.

That had been some time ago now, of course, and while the paper had been happy for him to ride on the back of the story's success for a while, he had known it wouldn't last forever. His regular column, "Brennan's Britain", had been the answer. Ostensibly a look at contemporary culture, he had been encouraged to use his weekly 1500 word allocation to express horror at the kinds of things he knew the paper's very specific kind of middle class, middle-aged readers would be similarly outraged by. Once he had exhausted such old standbys as linking movie violence and crime, immigration with unemployment, and video games with short attention spans, he found himself having to try harder to come up with things that would keep his column popular, and himself gainfully employed.

He hadn't had to look far to find the answer. In fact he hadn't had to look any further than the trunk he kept in his own attic, the one with three padlocks on that all required different combinations to get them open. He had always been worried that it might get discovered one day and so, embracing the philosophy that the best defence is a good offence, Michael Brennan had become a crusader against pornography. The pleasant, and thoroughly unexpected side effect of this, had been discovering that having a serious moral objection to such material also happened to be the best way of acquiring it. Some of his more enthusiastically horrified readers had directed him to the very best outlets, establishments and websites that purveyed the sickening material he was determined to expose for the nation's safety. Soon he found himself having to buy another trunk with the extra money the paper was now paying him, and that one was nearly full now as well. In fact, if he acquired any more 'specialist research material' he was going to have to think seriously about moving house.

And this girl he was currently following might just lead him to the story that would bag him the funds to buy one.

He could remember the letter she had sent him two weeks ago almost word for word. After all, he would use it to kick off the article he was intending to write, an article that would portray her as one of the poor helpless victims that he, crusading journalist Michael Brennan, had saved by exposing the immoral filth that was taking place and, worse, being filmed, at one of Britain's more out-of-the-way public schools.

Of course what she had put in her letters could also turn out to be nonsense, which is why he had agreed to meet her at the very place where she claimed the events were taking place. Well, not right at the school. His car was parked in a lay-by on an isolated country road a mile or so back, and he had walked the rest of the way, meeting her at the main entrance to the school by a pair of heavy iron gates painted green.

They had also been locked.

"It's the holidays," she had explained. "Don't you have kids of your own?"

Brennan had shaken his head, suddenly embarrassed that she thought him old enough to be her father. "But if that's the case why are you dressed like that?" he had asked.

A coquettish smile. "Because I've said I'll be in one of the films," she had whispered conspiratorially. "Term's only just ended, and my parents aren't expecting me back for another week, so I thought it would be the perfect time for us to work on this story together."

Brennan had groaned internally at her words. So that was it. She wanted her name on the piece too. Well, she was about to get her first hard lesson in the world of journalism, he thought, if all this came to anything.

The way in to the school grounds was through a much smaller gate further along. It led onto a dirt track that she had explained was only used by the school gardener. "When he's sober enough to drive that little cart of his," she had giggled.

Now they had been walking for nearly a quarter of an hour, and there was still no sign of anything remotely resembling a school.

"Nearly there," said the girl, skipping ahead as if daring him to chase after her, which he duly did, if only not to lose sight of where they were supposed to be going. They rounded a corner, and there was the school.

Brennan's first impression was to be distinctly underwhelmed. "It looks more like an old manor house," he said.

The girl shook her head. "It's nowhere near as old as it looks, or as old as its owners would like people to think. It's like a reproduction. My daddy calls it 'Stockbroker Tudor', whatever that means."

Brennan wasn't sure, but he made a point of remembering the phrase for his writeup.

"It's very quiet," he said, looking at the empty car park and the litter blowing around the deserted cricket pitches.

"Of course it is," said the girl. "I told you — term finished last week. Now come on."

The school's main doors were unlocked, and she led him into a high-ceilinged hallway with a pine floor so polished Brennan almost slipped. The wood panelling of the walls came up to waist height and had been painted a pale green. The white of the plaster above was all but obscured by numerous pin boards with green velvet backgrounds, documenting sporting fixtures and arrangements for end-of-term prize giving. Brennan nodded. If the locked gates and empty grounds had given him any doubts about this place being a real school they were gone now — only a madman would go to this level of detail to give an aura of authenticity.

"Well you've convinced me this is a school," he said, trying hard not to leer at the girl. She had unbuttoned her blazer now she was inside in the warm, and her white blouse was under a pleasurable degree of tension. "Now what?"

"Now you stay here, and wait for my signal," she said, skipping off down the corridor. Her regulation school shoes clattered on the wood as she rounded a corner, the sound of her footsteps vanishing as soon as she did. Brennan assumed the floor must be carpeted round there, and settled down to wait.

He wondered what her signal might be. Would she wait until they started filming? Or perhaps until she and whoever might be with her were, well, doing something his readers might consider morally outrageous? He licked his lips and hoped so, grateful for the digital camera that was nestling in his jacket pocket. He had carried one with him for the past two years, and it had got him a lot of 'worthwhile research material' in its time, so now he never travelled without it.

After fifteen minutes, he wondered if she was going to make a signal at all.

After twenty, he decided to find out what was going on for himself.

He was surprised to discover that the corridor she had turned into had the same kind of wooden floor tiles as where he had been standing, making him wonder why the sound of her footsteps had vanished so abruptly. Perhaps she had skipped quickly into one of the classrooms here, he thought. He made his way down the passageway, his own footsteps echoing noisily in the empty space, until he came to the first door. Set into its own little alcove on the left, the black letters on the anaemic green paint read: Mr K A Johnson — Mathematics.

Brennan listened at the door and, when he heard nothing, tried the brass meringue-shaped knob.

The door opened noiselessly to reveal the kind of classroom Brennan thought had gone out of style years ago. Twenty open-lid desks of the same polished pine as the floor tiles were arranged in five columns of four, all facing a large wooden table and chair that stood atop a wooden dais. Behind the chair, and to the right of it, an easel blackboard the colour of slate was propped on its wooden tripod, and held in place by three supporting pegs.

There was nothing written on the blackboard, no books on the master's desk, and not a soul in the room.

Except Brennan, of course.

He gave a cough and its echo cracked back at him. At least

the girl was telling the truth about it being school holidays, he thought, although he wondered what kind of pupils kept their desks so spotlessly clean, the lids unblemished by even the slightest suggestion of biro-etched graffiti or an ink-splattered fountain pen mishap.

The classroom of Mr J N Partleton — English, was a little further down the corridor on the right. It was arranged in the same way as Mr Johnson's and it, too, was empty.

You'd think they'd at least have some textbooks scattered around, Brennan thought, before realising the pupils probably had to buy their own and bring them along to lessons.

The next room on the left belonged to Mr M V Bradborough, who taught Geography. Brennan expected to see at least a globe or some maps on the walls, but the room was the same empty place of learning as the others.

He was about to give the final room in the corridor, the last door on the right, a miss, when there was a sound from behind it.

Brennan read the name on the door. Mr M Carmichael — Classics. Good God, did they still teach Latin and Greek these days? Brennan put his ear to the door. Yes, there was definitely something going on in there. It was faint, but as he concentrated he thought he could make out words.

No, not words.

Chanting.

Boys' voices, chanting Latin.

Increasingly furious at the thought that his time was being wasted, Brennan yanked open the door to confront the Latin summer school or whatever the hell it was.

The classroom was empty.

That was impossible! He had heard them!

Brennan strode inside and looked around. The room was like all the others — no books, no teacher, no pupils.

Nothing.

The voices had stopped now as well. In fact, Brennan realised, they had stopped as soon as he had come through the door.

"Ah! I see we have a new pupil in the class!"

Brennan whirled to see a figure standing in the doorway, a figure clad in a worn dark suit. A pocket watch had been tucked into the fraying pocket of the man's waistcoat. The mortarboard had seen better days as well, and the black teacher's gown had smears of chalk dust here and there from times when the blackboard rubber had probably been hidden by an especially mischievous pupil, or misplaced in a moment of absent-mindedness.

This new arrival peered at Brennan through a pair of tiny rimless spectacles. Vision through the circular lenses must have been almost entirely obscured by the myriad tiny splintered cracks in the glass. Nevertheless Mr Carmichael, if it was he, seemed to have no trouble seeing Brennan.

"Well answer me, boy," he said, taking a step forward and closing the door behind him. "I don't know where you were before, but here, if a master asks you a question, you answer. Promptly, politely, and respectfully."

Brennan was so shocked he found himself momentarily lost for words.

"Who the hell are you?" he eventually managed to stammer.

"Oh my," said Mr Carmichael. "That won't do. That won't do at all."

In the corner by the door was what looked like an umbrella stand, but instead, it housed a collection of what looked like very thin walking sticks. Carmichael took a step to his left, and as he drew one out, Brennan realised they weren't walking sticks at all.

They were canes.

"I can see we're going to have to teach the new boy a lesson," said Carmichael to no-one that Brennan could see. He gave the cane a couple of experimental swishes through the air, once to the right and once to the left, as if he was preparing for a fencing duel rather than the delivery of corporal punishment. Then he pointed at the table with it.

"I suggest you make yourself ready, young man."

Brennan was about to splutter an objection when Carmichael continued. "However, I see no reason why the misbehaviour of one especially bad apple should ruin this morning's lesson. Boys, continue with what we were doing while I deal with this miscreant. Second declension — begin."

Carmichael pressed a switch near the door. Suddenly the air around Brennan was filled with boys' voices, almost as if the classroom had become home to a Latin lesson for ghosts.

"Dominus, Domine, Dominum," the boys chanted as Carmichael advanced, the cane held high. Now he was closer, Brennan could see the tiny razor-sharp steel points that had been fitted along the length of rattan.

If he was hit with that it would open him up like a pig being gutted.

"Domini, Domino, Domino," the voices chanted as Brennan held up his hands.

"Now look," he said. "I'm sorry I'm trespassing, but I was led here under false pretences. I'm a journalist and — "

The cane descended, tearing into both of Brennan's outstretched palms. He screamed and took two steps back.

"Domini, Domini, Dominos," said the boys.

"For God's sake!" he screamed as Carmichael pursued him, the man raising his cane to deliver another blow. "I haven't done anything wrong!"

"Oh I wouldn't say that," said Carmichael. With a flick of the wrist he ripped open Brennan's right cheek, then the left, finishing off by making a deep gouge across the man's forehead.

"Dominorum, Dominis, Dominis," came the voices over the speakers as Brennan fell to his knees, blood streaming down his face. The chanting stopped as the man who had been beating him removed his spectacles.

"In fact, I'd say you've been a bad boy," he said, bringing his face close to Brennan's own beaten features. "A very, very bad boy indeed."

Through bloodstained vision, Brennan looked into the face of the man who, for no reason, had decided to torment him.

And then he realised that the man actually had a very good reason indeed.

"Valentine!" he croaked, his voice quaking with fear. He spat blood onto the otherwise spotless floor. "Oh my God."

"Not quite," said Edward Valentine. "But certainly someone sent to show you the error of your ways." He raised the cane for yet another attack, and then paused as he looked into the middle distance.

"That's very good, boys," he said. "Now — the third declension." Silence.

"Oh of course," said Valentine with a smile to the weeping mess that Brennan had become. "I have to change the tape. Excuse me."

As his tormentor went over to the doorway, Brennan realised this might be his only chance to escape. He pushed himself to his feet, bent his head down and, ignoring the dripping blood pooling on the floor, cannoned his body towards the door.

Valentine pushed another button.

As Brennan found himself in the corridor, more boys' voices surrounded him, coming from the speakers that had been set into the ceiling at regular intervals.

"Rex, rex, regem," the voices said as Brennan staggered towards the exit. He turned and through a bloody mist saw a caped figure close behind him.

"Regis, regi, rege," the boys chanted. Brennan ran back the way he had come and quickly found himself in the open air.

"Reges, reges, reges," came the voices from all around him, from the speakers set into the trees, into the walls of the building, from everywhere he looked.

"No escape for naughty boys," said Valentine from behind him. "And you, Mr Brennan, are a very naughty boy indeed."

From behind one of the trees that skirted the tennis courts appeared the girl who had first enticed him here. She waved to him.

"Come on!" she called, her tone urgent. "This way!"

"Regum, regibus, regibus," said the boys on the tape, concluding their latest task.

Brennan had no time to think and so he ran towards her, under the horizontal tree branch that arched ten feet over her head, and straight into the hangman's noose she looped over his head and tightened around his neck.

"What are you doing?" he said in choked tones as the girl backed away, leaving Brennan tethered by the rope that had been strung over the branch above him.

"She's doing what she was asked, Mr Brennan," said Valentine, coming up to the hapless journalist and raising the cane once more. "Now, can you remember the Latin for 'to love or to like'?"

Brennan started to cry, the mixture of blood and tears obscuring his vision entirely for a moment as he desperately tried to avoid another flogging.

"Amo! he said eventually in between the sobs. "Amo! It's amo!"

Valentine tutted. "I would have hoped that a man of your age and presumed education would have at least been able to present the verb in the classically accepted manner." He raised the cane as the man before him struggled. "Allow me to refresh your memory. The Latin verb for to like or to love is Amo — I love," he whipped the back of Brennan's neck. "Amare — to love," another slash across the face, "Amavi — I have loved," a hard blow across the back of the knees that caused Brennan to collapse, "and finally, Amatus, which is?"

Brennan didn't know, or he was bleeding too much to be able to answer. Valentine took hold of the end of the rope that had been coiled around the hook screwed into the back of the tree trunk. He unwound it, and began to pull.

The journalist was yanked to his feet, then to tiptoe, and then into the air.

"The supine stem!" Valentine said as he pulled the rope still further. Brennan, coughing, choking, his eyes watering, pulled at the constriction around his neck as he rose higher and higher.

Once he was satisfied, Valentine wound the rope around the hook once more before making his way round so that dying journalist could see him.

"I hope your education here this afternoon will allow you to at least understand me, Mr Brennan when I say Non Te Amo. Non Te Amo one little bit."

Dr Valentine and his companion watched Brennan's death throes together. Once he was satisfied that the journalist was dead, Valentine turned to the young lady beside him.

"I think that concludes our lesson for today," he said. She smiled back at him as he added, "And now, I think, for tea on the lawn."

They walked away from the hanging body of Michael Brennan, the man's torn face a mask of blood, his eyes glazed in death, hung out to dry like so many of those whom his column had shamefully and needlessly destroyed over the years.

But would no longer.

FIVE

This time the phone call came at at far more convenient time, and performed the useful function of getting John Spalding out of a preview screening of something low budget and intensely violent. At first he thought the surround sound had been cranked up a little too high before he realised the vibration in his pocket was the police trying to get hold of him again. Grateful though he was to be excused the cavalcade of blood-drenched atrocities being depicted on screen, he wasn't at all happy when it was explained what was required of him.

"You want me to go where?" he said.

"Bristol, sir." It was Martinus again. "Since we last spoke to you there's been another death, in another part of the country, and your name has cropped up as knowing him as well. Plus it would seem something happened a week or so ago that might involve you too. The investigation's become national, and it's been decided to base operations in Bristol. I've been asked to go along to supply information regarding the death of Margaret Upchurch, and they're requesting that you come along too."

Spalding shook his head in disbelief. "What are you talking about? Who else is dead?"

There was a pause on the other end of the line while Martinus presumably consulted his notes. "Earlier this morning a Mr Michael Brennan was found hanging from a tree in the grounds of a former public school in Buckinghamshire," he said. "And just over a week ago, near the A470 coming out of Cardiff a Mr David Bradshaw was found dead by the roadside."

Spalding could tell from the way Martinus broke off that there was obviously more. "He wasn't just found dead by the roadside, was he, Inspector?"

Again there was that pregnant pause that Spalding was starting to get used to. "No sir, he wasn't. Mr David Bradshaw was found impaled on a five foot high brass crucifix stolen from St David's Cathedral. So I hope you understand why I've sent someone round to where you were watching your film, sir."

Spalding looked up to see a uniformed police officer getting out of a squad car. "Yes I do, Inspector," was all he could say as he allowed himself to be led to the vehicle.

*

The Bristol police station meeting room Spalding was shown into was considerably bigger that the last room he had been questioned in. Windows at the far end looked out over a city that just then was bathed in late afternoon sunshine.

There were two other people in the room.

Spalding recognised Derek Martinus, and the young serious-looking woman with the short blonde hair turned out to be DI Susannah Graves from Cardiff. Apparently a DI Wentworth was coming over from Buckinghamshire as well, but he hadn't arrived yet. After the introductions, Spalding decided to be the one to break the ensuing awkward silence.

"So, do either of you know why I'm here?" he asked.

"Well," said Martinus, "you knew Margaret Upchurch."

"And," added Graves, "you knew Mr Bradshaw. Your number was in his phone. We didn't realise you might be connected to what was going on until your number also turned up on Michael Brennan's phone as well."

Spalding suppressed a nervous cough as he poured water from the jug on the table into an empty plastic cup. "Do you think I did it?" he said.

"In an ordinary case you'd be the prime suspect," said Martinus, clasping his hands on the table. "But this isn't ordinary."

Spalding frowned. "Then who do you think is responsible?"

"I'll tell you who's responsible," said a voice. "He was last seen heading over the Bristol Channel in a hot air balloon shaped like a giant raven."

DCI Jeffrey Longdon, late of the Avon and Somerset Constabulary, but very much recently reinstated and promoted, eyed the three of them from the doorway.

"And who saw him doing that?" said Spalding with a barely concealed chuckle of disbelief.

"I did, sunshine," said Longdon, stepping into the room, "and I very much hoped I would never hear his bloody name ever again." He waved an empty mug in their general direction. "Nice little job down in Cornwall, that was all I wanted. Nice bit of peace and quiet while I waited for my pension to come through. Maybe a bit of sheep rustling to sort out, the occasional bit of petty larceny or vandalism perhaps, but definitely not outrageously contrived deaths that no-one in their right mind would believe possible if they hadn't seen them with their own eyes. Which, of course, I have."

"Dr Valentine," Spalding breathed.

"Too right Dr Valentine, son, too bloody right." Longdon took one look at the water cooler and yelled out of the door. "For Christ's sake can't we get some coffee in here? I didn't come back to drink something from a bloody mountain spring. If I wanted that I'd have got a job in bloody Tibet."

Graves turned to Spalding. "You've heard of him, then?"

Spalding nodded. "Rather more than that I'm afraid." He looked at Longdon. "Can I use my smartphone in here?"

"Well I hope you can, son," Longdon looked as if he had just been asked something in ancient Greek, "because I certainly wouldn't know how to."

Spalding tapped the screen until the relevant site came up. Once he had found what he wanted he held the phone up to Longdon. "It's a book," he said.

Longdon peered at the picture on the screen.

"'The Nine Deaths of Dr Valentine'," he read, before giving Spalding an incredulous stare. "Are you telling me you wrote a book about that lunatic?"

"Not me, Inspector," said Spalding, passing the phone around so the others could also see the picture. "We. Once all the fuss had died down I contacted the journalists who covered the Dr Valentine story for the national dailies. I thought a book about his crimes might sell well, and that their input would be invaluable.

Unfortunately, because we could never agree how best to do it, it ended up being just a rehash of the original articles they wrote."

Longdon didn't seem impressed. "And what were these articles like?" he asked.

Spalding looked confused. "Like, Inspector?"

Longdon nodded. "Yes, like. I mean were they sensitive, well-researched, accurate?"

"Well I wouldn't quite say — "

"Or might they just have been given the usual tabloid treatment?" Longdon continued. "Might they just have been a little bit embellished? Sexed up? Made more appealing to the readers? In a word, Mr Spalding, might they have been what we in the force would refer to as Total Bollocks?"

"That's two words, Inspector," Spalding said, only to instantly regret it as Longdon gave him a look that could blast rivets through steel.

"Don't try my patience, sonny. I know what you do for a living, and no matter what you've seen on the cinema screen, it's nothing compared to what he did to all those doctors. Nothing." Longdon took a breath. The silence in the room was palpable. "What the hell were you lot all thinking?"

"The story was so popular it seemed the obvious thing to do," Spalding replied. "And I have to say the book did very well."

"Yes," said Longdon. "And I have to say that now it appears he's planning to do you lot 'very well', doesn't it? Did it never occur to you that we never caught him? Did it never even for a moment enter your heads that he might come back?"

"He was a wanted man, Inspector." Spalding was doing his best not to shout now. "What possible reason could he have had for wanting to come back here?"

"I think you and your friends have given him a perfect reason," said Longdon. He went over to the window and gazed out over the sun-blushed buildings. "A brilliant, rich, unstoppable psychopath, and you and your friends have gone and waved the biggest red flag anyone could ever conceive of right in his face. Well done. Well bloody done. It's because of you I'm not down in St Ives now checking that Mrs Humphries' Scone and Jam Shop hasn't decided to engage in a little bit of illegal Sunday trading, before popping over to the local for a pint."

"Where do we go from here, sir?" DI Graves looked at Longdon expectantly.

"The first thing we need to do," Longdon replied as he turned to face them once more, "is find out what he's basing the murders on this time."

"Isn't that a bit of an assumption, sir?" That was Martinus. "He might not be basing them on anything."

Longdon snorted. "A bloke run through with a massive crucifix? A girl wrapped in bandages soaked with embalming fluid?" No-one dared say a word. "The only I thing I am sure of so far is that it's not Vincent Price films this time. I had to watch nearly every bloody one of them two years ago and none of them have deaths like those in them."

"No," said Spalding with quiet confidence. "They don't."

All eyes turned to him.

"You say that as if you might know where they are from," said Longdon, his tone no longer quite so admonishing.

"I might," said Spalding. "You see, I don't think he's gone too far from his original inspiration."

"Well, out with it, lad," said Longdon, dragging up a chair.

"Even if it's ridiculous I'm more than willing to give it a serious listen at this point."

Spalding took a deep breath. "In the film *Dracula Has Risen From the Grave*, Christopher Lee, as Dracula, is finally killed at the end of the film by being dropped from a great height onto a huge metal crucifix."

"So it's films starring Christopher Lee this time," said Longdon. "At least that's a start." Spalding tried to interrupt but it was no good. "Can you put together a list for me of this bloke's most memorable film appearances, especially including ones where he — "

"It's not films starring Christopher Lee." Spalding eventually managed to shout Longdon down. It wasn't a pretty sight. "At least, not specifically him."

Longdon's eyes narrowed. "What do you mean?"

Spalding waited until he was sure the DCI was going to keep quiet before continuing. "In the film *Blood From the Mummy's Tomb* the character of Margaret, played by Valerie Leon, is crushed beneath a falling building and the final shot is of her wrapped in bandages pleading for help to the camera."

"And Christopher Lee's not in that one?" Graves asked.

"No, he's not." Spalding replied.

"Damn!" Longdon thumped the table. "So there's not going to be a pattern this time. It'll just be any old daft film he can think of."

"No Inspector, not just 'any old daft film'." Spalding was getting tired of having to fight for the stage but it was still most likely the quickest way he would be able to get out of here. "In the film *Fear In The Night* Ralph Bates is hanged from the branch of a tree in the grounds of a deserted public school, just like Michael Brennan."

"Is Christopher Lee in that?"

"No, Inspector, he's not."

"Or this Valerie girl you mentioned?"

"Inspector Longdon," Spalding said, getting to his feet, "do you want to know the link between these three films, or don't you?"

Longdon's eyes widened at that. "So there is a link?"

"Yes!" Now it was Spalding's turn to thump the table in frustration. "Good God, man, I'm trying to tell you! All three movies were made by Hammer Films, arguably the most famous British picture company ever!"

"I thought that was Ealing," said Derek Martinus.

"Shut up, DI Martinus." Longdon turned back to Spalding. "You've got a good point there, son, I'll give you that. What better way to bump off a load of British journalists you hate than by using a British institution like that."

"Are Hammer Films a British institution?" asked DI Graves from the back.

"Even I've heard of them," said Longdon. "Therefore they must be." Then it was back to Spalding. "Can you give me a list of their key films?"

Spalding sat down again, leaned back in his chair and rolled his eyes. "I could give it a go," he said. "But it would go on for several pages."

"Doesn't matter," said Longdon with a shake of his head. "If it's one thing I learned from my previous encounter with our Dr Valentine, it's that he's nothing if not obsessive. Get me that list, and somewhere on it will be what he's planning next. In the meantime," he said to Spalding," I also need a list of everyone who contributed to that book of yours."

"It shouldn't be too difficult to remember," Spalding replied, taking out a pen to scribble on the notepad Longdon had just handed him. "After all, there aren't too many of them left."

He ignored the inspector's expression as he did his best to remember everyone who had contributed to the book, and was still alive. By the time Spalding had finished he was sure he had all of them, except perhaps one.

Spalding stared at the list of names in front of him and willed himself to remember the one that was missing. It was a woman, wasn't it? A woman who had written for the Daily Express, or possibly The Sun, he couldn't remember which. Spalding drummed his fingers on the table while the others waited. Longdon had sent out for a copy of the book but Spalding knew it would be quicker if he could just remember.

Her name was on the tip of his tongue.

For Christ's sake, he thought. What was it?

SIX

"Fran?"

Francesca Warren stopped stirring her coffee, an action she had been performing for the better part of the last five minutes, and looked over to see who had shouted to her from the door of the coffee shop.

Oh God, she thought, it was Yvonne Carstairs, the very last person she needed to see right now.

Fran had been 'friends' with Yvonne for the past six months or so. She always thought of the term in inverted commas because, as far as she was concerned, people in the media didn't have real friends so much as people they could use to get the next gig, and that was certainly how the two of them treated each other. Fran didn't mind that — it was just the sort of thing one did if one wished to get on. What she did mind was the woman herself. Yvonne was chirpier, prettier, but worst of all, younger — something Fran had never been able to forgive her for. Even though Yvonne had yet to achieve the kind of success Fran had enjoyed with the Dr Valentine thing, she was sure it would come. Meanwhile, Fran was spending far too many hours in coffee shops wondering if her five greatest column inches of fame were already behind her.

"I thought it was you." Yvonne had already glided across the room, effortlessly avoiding the messy three year old in the buggy (she had dealt it and the child's mother the kind of understanding look that had her interviewees opening up in spades, and how Fran hated her for it), and with a swish of her white knee length Louis Vuitton skirt the girl was sitting beside her. Whether Fran wanted her there or not.

"Hello Yvonne," Fran said, forcing a smile and putting down the spoon she might do something silly with if the other girl said the wrong thing. "How's the world of fashion?"

"Oh, much the same." Yvonne accompanied the words with the sigh of mock boredom that all her kind seemed to acquire once they had been let loose on unsuspecting Paris couturiers. "How about you?"

Fran tried to imitate Yvonne, but instead of evoking a sense of chic ennui, her sigh just came out sounding vaguely depressed. "Fine, fine," she said, in a way that meant it was anything but.

"Oh you poor love." Yvonne folded her hands in her lap and leaned forward. "Tell me all about it."

Of course, Fran couldn't really do that. Any chink in the journalist's armour, especially the female journalist, would just get widened and ripped into by her female colleagues. So she put away thoughts of her latest relationship breakup, and the consequent loss of the possible headlining story she had been using him to get to, and elected to remain non-committal.

"Just the usual, darling," she said, drawling on the last word with all the false sincerity of many years of practice. "Men. And editors. And anything else you'd care to suggest."

"Oh no!" Fran knew that Yvonne wasn't really the slightest bit concerned, but she was capable of putting on an exemplary job of pretence. "Editors can be a bitch sometimes, can't they?"

Fran nodded, grateful the conversation had been skilfully diverted into something they could both have a nice, manageable non-specific moan about. "They can," she replied. "And the women are even worse!"

They both giggled at that. Fran sipped coffee. Yvonne looked at her watch.

"Are you in a hurry?" Fran asked, hoping that the other girl was.

"Kind of," Yvonne replied. "In fact, it's absolutely serendipitous me finding you here. You couldn't do me the most enormous favour, could you?"

Fran's ears pricked up at that. Any favour could always be exploited. "That depends what it is," she said, smiling sweetly. "But you know I'll always do my best to help."

Yvonne leaned further forward and lowered her voice to a conspiratorial whisper. "Well," she said. "You know that lovely young model I've been exhausting most nights?"

Fran didn't, but she nodded enthusiastically anyway. "Of course!" she lied, determined to get more information in case she could use it later. "What did you say his name was again?"

Was it Fran's imagination, or did the other girl's cheeks blush a little pinker at that? "It's not a he, my love. That's why I've had to keep it absolutely one hundred percent quiet. You know how people wouldn't understand."

Fran nodded, doing her best to rein in her excitement. People certainly wouldn't understand, not in the industry and certainly not the readership of middle England. In fact they'd not understand to the point of at least wanting to read about it all on page three, or even page one if it was a slow news day. Fran reached over and gave Yvonne's wrist a squeeze that was tight with empty reassurance.

"What can I do?" she said.

"Well." Yvonne licked her lips. Was this difficult for her? How delicious! "We've been having a bit of trouble, and so I've arranged for us to meet up this afternoon. The problem is, that bloody editor of mine has set up an interview that I'm supposed to be doing at the same time." Yvonne looked at the now infinitely superior-feeling Fran with wide eyes. "You couldn't possibly do the interview for me, could you?"

Fran let a few deliciously painful seconds pass as she pretended to think about it. She stroked her chin, gazed off into the middle distance, and generally milked the moment for all it was worth before answering.

"I've quite a bit of work lined up this afternoon myself," she lied. "But, yes, of course I'll do it. What are friends for?"

"Oh, thank you!" The girl seemed genuinely grateful and, for a moment, Fran felt almost guilty for revelling in her misery. Almost. "It's a new company." Yvonne was already searching in her bag. "The magazine wants me to interview their managing director, get the lowdown on their products, philosophy, all that sort of thing." It took a bit of struggling but eventually Yvonne produced a slightly creased business card.

Fran peered at the elegant font.

" 'Ayesha Industries' " she read. " 'Come And Bathe In Our Eternal Flame'."

"That's their new cosmetics line," Yvonne explained. "They're launching it next month."

Fran tucked the card away. "Well it's nothing if not dramatic," she said.

Yvonne nodded. "That's what I thought. They could be the next big thing. To be honest I'm probably shooting my career in the head not taking it myself, but I really can't. Are you still happy to do it?"

Oh yes, Fran was happy all right. Fran was bloody ecstatic.

"Only if you're absolutely sure," she said, crossing her fingers.

"Oh I am," said Yvonne, already getting to her feet. "Thank you so much. You'll never know how much this means to me."

Perhaps not, thought Fran. But I just might do my best to find out. "Don't worry, darling," she said. "Fran will take care of everything."

There was no answer to that and so, after brushing lips against both cheeks the two women parted. When Yvonne had gone, Fran allowed herself a little chuckle as she looked at the card once more. A cosmetics interview, she thought, blessing her good luck. What could possibly go wrong?

*

The offices and distribution warehouse of Ayesha Industries were located in an industrial park on the south side of Nottingham. A tiny map showing the establishment's exact location was printed on the back of their business card. Fran also liked the little optical trick the company had thought to include on the front. Next to the company name and slogan was a picture of the face of a beautiful girl. That wasn't so surprising, but if you held the card up to the light and angled it just so the picture changed to that of a haggard old lady.

Cute, Fran had thought, and it was also a decent little bit of manipulation. Show the customer what she thought she looked like now, and what she would look like after Ayesha Cosmetics had finished with her. At least that was what she presumed it was intended to convey, but it hadn't been terribly well made — the 'before' and 'after' pictures seemed to be the wrong way around.

She parked her two-seater BMW in the empty car park, got out and looked around. The place seemed deserted for a Wednesday afternoon. Then she remembered the numerous 'To Let' signs she had seen on the way in. That didn't bode well. If Ayesha Cosmetics could only afford to set up in a place where industrial property prices were at a minimum, she wondered if they might have cut corners with 'Eternal Flame' as well.

She pushed the buzzer to the left of the glass panelled door labelled 'Office', noting as she did so that at least the sign looked as if it had been professionally put together. The red-lettered gothic font on a black background felt a little severe for a company that was trying to present itself as the future of beauty, but that was just something else she could write about.

Fran didn't have to wait long for an answer. She did, however, have to pause for a moment to take in what the individual who opened the door was wearing. She thought pink could look all right on a man if it was just a shirt, but an entire suit and tie to match was going over the top a bit.

No, she thought, stifling a giggle. A lot.

"Miss Carstairs?" the man's overly bouffanted Liberace hairstyle gleamed silver in the afternoon sun, but the swathes of lacquer in which the locks seemed to have been coated prevented the slight breeze from disturbing its almost mathematical perfection.

Fran shook her head. "Yvonne couldn't come," she said, extending a hand and giving him her most winning smile. "I'm Francesca Warren."

His grip was oddly synthetic. Probably the result of too much all-over body Botox, she guessed. When he smiled the corners of his face looked as if they might fold in on themselves. Definitely Botox, she thought.

"How lovely to meet you, Miss Warren," he replied. "I'm sorry your colleague couldn't come, but I'm delighted that she managed to find someone even more beautiful to come in her stead. I am Dr Chantler Day, managing director and indeed founder of Ayesha Cosmetics. And my, do I have some intoxicating things to show you this afternoon."

I'll believe that when I see it, Fran thought as she followed him inside. Still, she had to give him full marks for being a quirky character, and they were always so much easier to write about.

Dr Day led her down the length of a narrow brightly-lit corridor. At the far end stood a pale olive coloured door, next to which was a numeric key pad. He paused and turned to her.

"Do you wish to see what lies behind the green door, Miss Warren?"

Fran shrugged. "Of course," she said. "That's what I'm here for."

Dr Day's eyes tried to crease for a second, in spite of whatever treatments he had applied to the skin around them, before he typed in a number on the pad. There was a woosh of air as the door opened.

"Air tight," he explained. "But don't worry, the room is fully air conditioned in a very special way that I'll explain in a minute."

Fran suddenly had visions of being pushed into this air tight room by this strange man and she held back.

"There's nothing to be afraid of here!" Dr Day chuckled. "But if it makes you feel any better, I'll go in first."

The room inside was surprisingly large and echoingly bare. White walls and a white ceiling added to the atmosphere of sterility, and the air from the vent in the ceiling had a strange, ozone-like smell to it.

"Please take a seat." Day motioned to the chair positioned in front of the remarkably elaborate makeup counter that was the room's only other item of furniture.

"Where are you going to sit?" Fran asked, putting her bag down and positioning herself before the makeup mirror. Christ, she looked a bit rough today.

Day stood behind her and put his hands on her shoulders. "I shall not be sitting," he said. "I shall be showing you the magic of Eternal Flame."

Fran craned her neck to look at him, but Day gently but firmly turned her head so she could only see his reflection as he towered over her. "You're not going to give me a makeover, are you?" she said, looking at her own image again and rather hoping he was.

"Not just a makeover," said Day. "I am going to turn you into a different woman. Believe me, by the time you walk out of here you will feel as you never have before."

"Well, not to cast aspersions on you or your products," Fran said, wrinkling her nose, "but that's going to a hell of thing to try and pull off."

"Nevertheless," Day said, his hands still on her shoulders, "I very much feel that today I shall achieve it. Now, the first thing I need for you to do is to take a deep breath." In case she wasn't sure of his instruction, he demonstrated it for her.

Fran did as she was told, and again that was that slight sting in her nostrils. "Why?" she asked.

"Do you know one of the main threats to beauty?" Day asked, his face grave. "One of the worst things to harm beautiful skin, the perfection of youth?"

Fran shrugged. She couldn't imagine he was going to come up with anything revolutionary, but she let him have his moment.

Dr Day raised his arms and looked up at the ceiling. "Why, the very air itself!" His gaze snapped back down to regard her. "Did you know that air is mainly made of nitrogen? Nitrogen filled with bacteria and dust particles, toxins and poisons, all of them quite, quite terrible for your pores?" Fran knew what air was made of but she kept quiet. "That is why we insist that Eternal Flame cosmetics be applied in a pure oxygen environment. What you are breathing in at the moment is not common air, Miss Warren, but one hundred percent pure and unsullied oxygen! It's used in hospitals all the time to treat patients with breathing problems. All I am doing is using it on the beautiful to make them even more so!"

Okay, Fran thought, so he's a little bit potty. In fact he might be quite a lot potty. Did she trust him to put stuff on her face?

She needed the article.

"Okay," she said, cautiously. "But surely if this makeup has to be applied in this sort of atmosphere, you're shooting yourself in the foot with the home cosmetics market?"

"Ayesha Products will not be for home use," Day explained. "They will be salon only. It will increase their exclusivity, and therefore their popularity."

Just another fad then. But that was fine. Fads made good copy. In fact the more over the top, the better. Fran gave him a regal wave.

"In that case, carry on, maestro," she said with a wry grin.

Day clapped his hands. They made a curiously dull sound. "Excellent! Now, first we need to apply the foundation. If you would be kind enough to look up and close your eyes."

He reached over her shoulder and took a small unlabelled aerosol canister from the table. He shook it twice and then, holding it at arm's length, proceeded to spray a liberal quantity of it in the air above Fran's upturned face. She coughed, and then grimaced as the particles began to settle on her skin.

"I wasn't expecting perfume," she said.

Dr Day shook his head. "I didn't say it was, Miss Warren. It's an entirely new concept in foundation makeup. The substance I have applied to your face and neck and now..." he added another couple of squirts "...to your hands, is a fast acting foundation and moisturiser combined. Do you feel anything?"

Fran opened her eyes. "Now that you mention it," she said, "my skin does feel kind of tingly."

The beauty specialist clapped his hands. "Excellent! In that case, we're ready to move onto the next stage. If you will allow me." He placed his hands on Fran's shoulders and swung the swivel chair round so she was facing him. "All you need to do now is let me work my magic, and then you'll have the most amazing story to write about."

Fran remained unconvinced as the man began to — rather inexpertly — apply a blusher of an unflattering shade to her cheeks, followed by some glittery lilac eyeshadow that she thought had gone out of style thirty years ago. Still, the eighties were supposed to be coming back, and she supposed she should wait for the overall effect.

"Oh my," said Dr Day as he applied what felt like swathes of the stuff, "you really are looking hot, young lady." He uncapped a lipstick of an especially violent purple hue. "Yes," he said, pausing, his voice lowering in tone. "Very hot indeed. Tell me, Miss Warren, have you ever been hauled over the coals?"

Fran frowned. "What?"

"Oh nothing, nothing," came the reply, almost as if the mask she imagined was now firmly back in place had never actually slipped. "I was just thinking." He began to apply the waxy substance to her mouth. "The kind of job you do, you must have given some people a rough ride in the past. In your articles I mean."

"It's all part of the job," said Fran. "To tell the truth, to give the public what they want."

"That's not always the same thing though, is it?" The voice had dropped in tone again. "The public don't always want the truth, do they? They want to be entertained, to be told a story, a story with a happy ending that can let them sleep in their beds at night, safe in the knowledge that at least it's not they who have been raked through the mud and filth of what passes for journalism nowadays."

"What are you on about?" Fran tried to stand, but her limbs felt unnaturally heavy.

"You're not drugged, in case you're wondering." The man's entire demeanour was different now, and the man himself seemed to have changed into someone much more serious. "It's something rather more effective than that."

Fran suddenly felt very scared. "What do you mean?" she said in a very small voice.

"Just a taste of your own medicine, Miss Warren." The man was peeling off the fine latex coverings that sheathed his hands. Now he was picking away the paper thin substance that he had used to coat his face. "You see, that's my specialty. Medicine, that is. Or rather, it was. Yours on the other hand is being paid money to tell lies about people who have had quite enough turmoil in their lives already."

Now he was lifting off that absurd hairpiece to reveal a visage that made Fran want to cry and go running to her mother. She was so terrified she could scarcely utter his name, but she managed it somehow, the word coming out as little more than a whisper.

"Valentine."

"Dr Valentine or, to be even more accurate, Mr Valentine, if you would be so kind. Although your sort rarely are, are they? Kind, I mean." There was barely-concealed malice in his voice now. "Which is partly why I've had to got to all this trouble and expense to teach you a lesson, to make you an example to your kind that you cannot just write what you like, and think you can get away with it."

Her heart filled with dread, Fran forced herself round to see what she looked like in the mirror.

And breathed a sigh of relief.

She looked ridiculous, certainly, as if someone with little or no experience had tried to make her up, but she wasn't scarred, she wasn't bleeding, and she wasn't teetering on the brink of a painful death.

She was, however, very angry.

She spun back round to face him. "I don't know if you think this is funny," she snapped, "but you've wasted an afternoon of my time with this little charade of yours, and so let me assure you that I certainly will be writing about it. And about you. Again."

Valentine merely shook his head and tutted. "You don't watch many horror films, do you, Miss Warren? I'm presuming this because, if you did, you'd know what happens to the victim who calls the villain of the piece all sorts of unpleasant names. Let me assure you that it never ends well."

Fran already had a tissue out and was rubbing at her makeup. Which wasn't shifting.

"It won't come off," said Valentine. "Not until you leave this room, anyway."

Fran stood up. "Then that's what I'm going to do," she said. "Right now."

Valentine stepped to one side and gestured to the door. "By all means," he said, "although I should probably warn you before you do."

"Why?" Fran sneered. "Have you got an axe waiting to drop on me on the other side? Or a pit waiting to open up?"

"Nothing so lacking in finesse for one so beautiful," he said, with a smile that had no humour in it. "You may remember I mentioned this room is being supplied with pure oxygen?" Fran nodded. "That's because the substance I have applied to your face reacts with the nitrogen in air, turning it into a highly corrosive acid. You cannot leave this room, Miss Warren. Ever."

Fran snorted. "That's ridiculous," she said. "You must have got some of the stuff on you when you were spraying me!"

"Indeed I did," Valentine replied. "Hence the need for the protective coverings you have just seen me remove. It takes a couple of minutes for the spray to combine with your skin, and then it's fixed there. Permanently." He took two steps towards the door. "And so now I hope you can understand why it is I who am going to leave this room and not you. The door is airtight and I've arranged for the oxygen to last for another half an hour or so. After that you get to decide whether you breathe your last in here or..."

"Why were you going to do this to Yvonne?" Fran cried, trying to decide if this madman was telling the truth. "She never wrote anything about you."

"She never wrote anything about anyone," said Valentine as the door opened and the familiar face of Fran's 'friend' appeared on the other side. "In fact she never wrote anything at all. You see," he said as he and the young woman exchanged smiles, "Yvonne is a very good friend of mine. Although I know her under a different name."

"Yvonne!" Fran screamed, on her feet but uncertain if it was safe to proceed any further, "help me!

"Oh no, darling," said the woman Fran had thought she knew well enough to trust. "You've only yourself to blame for this. I would say 'see you later' but we both know that's not going to happen."

The door swung shut with an air-tight hiss, leaving Fran to ponder her fate. Her only company was the noise from the air vent, and she knew that would be stopping soon enough.

She looked at herself in the mirror, and rubbed an experimental finger across her face. Her skin felt strange, but not exceptionally so. The stuff was all over her hands as well, like a fine coating of lacquer. Was it really capable of dissolving flesh? And there was so little of it, just the faintest trace, really. She couldn't accept that it was capable of doing what Valentine had said.

He just meant for her to suffocate, didn't he?

Fran got to her feet again, angry now that she should have been conned by such a cheap trick. She strode to the door. It had better be locked, Valentine, she thought, because if it isn't I'm coming after you.

The door opened with a sucking sound.

Fran hesitated, then took a single step into the corridor.

Another.

And another.

She looked at her hands.

Nothing.

Fran took several deep breaths and laughed out loud. That bastard! How dare he scare her like that!

She strode back the way she had come, determined to catch Valentine and that bitch Yvonne to give them both a piece of her mind before she got back to her keyboard to annihilate both of them on paper.

The door at the end of the corridor opened easily and Fran stepped into the open air of the car park.

At first she felt almost nothing, just a slight tingling as if her extremities had been numbed. Then there was not just pain, but searing, burning agony eating into her skin and burrowing into the deeper tissues beneath. Fran raised her right hand to see the flesh had already dissolved from the fingertips, revealing nubs of white bone that were already beginning to be eaten away before her eyes. She turned to run back the way she had come, but the door was now closed and locked, the company logo replaced by a sheet of paper on which were typed six words:

Pure oxygen in the corridor too!

They were the last thing she ever saw. As Fran clawed at the melting flesh of her face with fingertips of bleached crumbling bone she wondered if there would be anything left of her for the police to recover.

There was, but not very much.

SEVEN

The ceiling was ribbed and vaulted, and perfectly suited the drawing room of the elegantly appointed country house for which it had been constructed. The beautiful cornice work, always in shadow these days, rose twenty feet above the oak floor tiles, which were themselves over a hundred years old.

The room was almost in darkness, the bright sunshine of the day outside kept away by the heavy red velvet curtains that had been drawn across the double bay windows. The only illumination afforded this chamber was a single bare bulb burning above the pipe organ that took up the entire wall opposite.

The organ had two manuals. Its owner had initially wished for three, but to include a choir manual as well as the swell and the great would have meant extra expense that he had preferred to spend on other things. Right now he was playing Bach's Prelude in E Minor with an arrangement of stops so gentle it was best appreciated in otherwise absolute silence.

The man to the left who was currently bound to a wooden chair was preventing that.

The owner seemed not to mind, but it was difficult to tell because of the mask he wore. It was a rough, papier mache affair, that concealed his left eye and left a gap for his nostrils but not his mouth. Every now and then his right eye darted to his helpless victim, the eyelid creasing with annoyance. He should have anaesthetised this one as well as gagged him.

The music came to an end, and almost immediately the door opened. It was a heavy piece that dated back to the seventeenth century and had been imported from France. Despite its age, the excellent condition of it hinges and heavy floor runner had meant that some considerable time had been spent on making it creak appropriately.

A beautiful girl stood in the doorway. The same beautiful girl who, over the past couple of weeks, had posed as a socialite, a taxi driver, a schoolgirl, and finally and most recently as fashion writer Yvonne Carstairs, friend of the now late Francesca Warren.

The figure at the organ turned and acknowledged her presence. She in turn glanced at their latest prisoner, the poor man mistakenly taking her for a potential saviour. The pleading in his eyes was wasted on her.

"You've decided, then?" she said, as the phantom altered the combination of organ stops.

She was rewarded with a shake of the head as Valentine peeled off the mask. His suit was about fifty years out of date but was no less immaculate for it.

"I'm afraid not," he replied, before playing a few bars of something infinitely more threatening and definitely more flamboyant. He stopped and gave the man in the chair a worryingly insane look.

"Tony and I have been having a little chat, haven't we Tony?"

The man mumbled something in reply. The girl removed the gag and the words "My name's not Tony" tumbled from his tear-stained lips.

"Of course it isn't," said the girl. "That's not the point, silly. That's not the point at all." She looked back at the man sitting on the organ stool. "You couldn't decide, then?"

Valentine picked up the tattered mask. "Between *Phantom of the Opera* and *Paranoiac*? No, I'm afraid I couldn't. But as we're both aware, the time for procrastination is at an end. The police are not exactly closing in, but I would imagine they are at least trying to get themselves organised now. I'd be very disappointed if they weren't."

"Really?" said the girl.

Valentine nodded. "We've left them enough clues," he said. "That last one was the most obvious of all. Plus we made sure we left plenty of the 'Ayesha Cosmetics' business cards lying close to what little was left of poor Miss Warren. Anyone with access to a search engine should be able to work out her death was inspired by the film *She*." He gazed off into the distance. "You know," he said, "I wouldn't be at all surprised if the police are watching poor Ursula Andress dissolve in front of Peter Cushing and that other chap right now." He chuckled. "I wonder if they've dragged Inspector Longdon back from wherever he probably thought he'd been sent to live out his days. It would be rather delicious if he happened to be in charge of things again."

"Who are you?" the sobbing man in the chair asked the girl. "Why would you want to help him?"

Valentine answered for her. "I'm afraid even I don't know her real name," he said. "Either because she cannot remember it, or because she would prefer not to say. Whichever the reason may be I have always respected it, and have no intention of prying further. Suffice to say I call her Christina, because of the circumstances under which we met."

"He rescued me, you see," said Christina. "I had jumped from a very great height into a very deep body of water with the full intention of killing myself." She gave Valentine an apologetic look. "For reasons I have no intention of elaborating upon. Not just for now, anyway. It was only when I surfaced for the third time that I realised that it was not my time to die yet. And that was when I saw the raven."

The man looked confused. Bloody and tearstained as well, but mostly confused. "Raven?" he asked.

Valentine nodded. "A little affectation of mine," he said. "My escape route from the forces of the law, as well as a little flamboyant flourish to signify that my revenge was at an end. Something you and your friends have regrettably caused me to realise is not the case. Not the case at all."

"He picked me up in his balloon." For the first time since she had entered the room Christina smiled. It was utterly bewitching. "A strange man in a huge raven-shaped balloon saved my life. How could I not help him after that?"

"But that's a great story," the man spluttered. "You could sell that alone and get twenty thousand for it. I could arrange it for you, if you like."

"Be quiet, Tony," said Valentine.

"Yes, shut up, Tony," Christina added, pulling the gag back up for good measure. "Was it a good idea bringing him here?" she asked Valentine.

The doctor shrugged. "No-one saw him, and we go out so often. I rather liked the idea of entertaining at home for a change."

"True." The girl was making her way across the room now. "Well, if we're staying in, would you care for some champagne?"

Valentine nodded but held up a hand. "Afterwards, though," he said. "Nothing takes the chill out of good champagne more than excessive screaming."

Christina smiled again. "So you'd better hurry up and choose," she said. "Are you going to be Herbert Lom or Oliver Reed?"

Valentine pondered for moment, and then a brainwave struck. His eyes were gleaming when he next looked at her.

"Neither," he said, producing the syringe he had been intending to use anyway when his patient got a bit too noisy. "I'm going to be Eric Porter. Get the car while I make a couple of telephone calls."

*

"Before you go up, I just need to warn you that you can't take photographs in here."

The man in the cloak and pointed beard sighed at the words, and gestured with his silver-headed cane to the semi-conscious man propped up by the pretty nurse.

"I am not here to take pictures, young man," he said. "I am here in a final and desperate attempt to cure this poor young man of his inner demons!"

The elderly ticket vendor of the Whispering Gallery at St. Paul's Cathedral scratched his chin. "Oh yes," he said, adjusting the name badge that stated his name was Ronald. "We did receive a phone call about you earlier from someone high up in the Royal College of Psychiatrists. Will you be able to manage, Dr Pritchard, or would you like me to locate some assistance?"

The man calling himself Dr Pritchard shook his head. "Thank you," he said, "but we should be fine. Nurse Laura and I will ensure that he gets up there safely."

"Come on Mr Hannah," the girl said firmly, propelling the man in the direction of the stone spiral staircase. "You know this is for your own good."

"He doesn't look very well," said Ronald as Mr Hannah groaned and tried to resist the ministrations of his two carers.

"Of course he isn't well!" said Pritchard as his patient was helped onto the first step. "That's why we've brought him here, why he's had to be sedated, and why we really cannot be kept chatting when we have important work to do."

"Oh of course," said the little old man, staying with them rather than shuffling back to his ticket booth. "You're sure you don't need any help?"

"No."

Mr Hannah groaned and reached out an arm to the ticket vendor.

"I could call an ambulance if you like," the man added.

Pritchard and Nurse Laura had managed to get the man onto the third step now.

"Thank you," said the doctor, putting away the syringe he had just used to administer something to the poor man, "but that won't be necessary. At least not right now. If my patient does anything silly I can assure you that you will be the first to know."

Mr Hannah, suddenly more cooperative now he had received his injection, allowed himself to be manhandled the rest of the way as Ronald the ticket vendor, mumbling to himself all the while, made his way back to attend to a group of Spanish tourists who had just entered the building.

He had just finished the long and laborious process of selling individual tickets to all thirty of them, when there was a muffled thump from behind him.

He didn't need to turn round to know that something quite catastrophic had happened, something that caused most of the tourist group to run screaming from the building. But he did anyway, giving the broken body of poor suicidal Mr Hannah a cursory glance before turning back and calmly announcing to the few visitors remaining that the cathedral would need to be closed for the rest of the afternoon.

As he put the 'Closed' sign on his desk, Ronald realised he was going to need to ring for an ambulance after all.

EIGHT

"Are you telling me you didn't suspect anything?"

Longdon had taken the next available train to London while DI Martinus, DI Graves, and DI Colin Wentworth, who had finally turned up from Buckinghamshire, had been despatched elsewhere. John Spalding had insisted he accompany Longdon, partly because he thought being present at the crime scene might help spark some suggestion as to where Valentine might strike next, but mainly because he no longer felt safe on his own.

"I've told you twice." Ronald Turner-Wyatt was unhappy at having been kept behind at St Paul's so late, and he had already explained to the police officers that his cat Mungo was going to be even more unhappy about the delay in getting his dinner. "He was a doctor."

Longdon sighed. "And how did you know he was a doctor?" he asked.

"Well for a start," the little man replied, "he said he was one."

"Oh that's marvellous." Longdon's spell in Cornwall hadn't helped his diplomacy skills. "And if I told you I was the Queen of Sheba, would you believe that?"

Ronald shook his head. "You haven't got a crown," he said, before adding with a sniff, "besides — you're not a lady."

"He's got a point, Inspector." Spalding was gazing up at the gallery and marvelling at the distance from the balcony to the floor.

"That's enough from you," Longdon snapped. Behind the three of them the lifeless broken remains of Valentine's latest victim was being lifted onto a stretcher. Even ten feet away it was possible to hear the man's broken bones crunching as the fractured pieces jarred against one another. Longdon tried to cover up the noise with the sound of his own voice. "Why else did you think he was a doctor?"

"He had a patient with him," Ronald said. He looked over Longdon's shoulder as the flattened, vaguely man-shaped outline beneath the red blanket was wheeled away. "Poor man. Poor, poor man."

"Didn't he ask you for help?" Longdon was getting nowhere but he persisted anyway. "Didn't he try to tell you he was in danger?"

Ronald shook his head. "He wasn't very well at all. Dr Pritchard said he wasn't. Said he was troubled with all sorts and that they were going to help him clear his head."

"Well they did that all right, didn't they?" Longdon rolled his eyes. "They cleared his head clean off."

"He had permission from the Royal College of Psychiatrists." Ronald was indignant now and was showing signs of having had quite enough. "I don't know what else you want me to tell you, Inspector. He seemed a perfectly charming gentleman. A little eccentric, perhaps, what with that top hat and cane, but charming nevertheless. I can't believe they meant that poor man harm. I mean my goodness, even the nurse who was with him was lovely, and the essence of politeness."

Longdon's eyes blazed at that nugget of information and it was all he could do not to grab the little old man by the lapels. "What nurse?" he said, his voice barely a whisper.

"The one who was with him. Lovely girl. Really pretty. And just as well spoken as he was. Lovely couple they were. Shame you don't get to see more well-dressed people like that around these days."

Longdon did his best to remain calm as he put an arm around Ronald and pointed to a young man standing close to where the body had recently lain. He was making notes on a sketch pad. "Mr Turner-Wyatt, you've been of the utmost help to us," said the Inspector, "and I cannot begin to tell you how grateful we all are for you giving us some of your valuable time."

"Mungo won't be happy," Ronald said again.

Longdon ignored him. "All I need you to do before you leave is have a word with Steve over there. I want you to give him as accurate a description of this girl as you can. He'll draw it for you as you go along and I want you to stop him and get him to change it if what he draws isn't exactly like the nurse you saw here this afternoon. Do you understand?"

"I really have to be going."

"I understand that, Mr Turner-Wyatt, I really do. But you see, it's vitally important that we find her as her life could be in danger."

Ronald seemed to wake up at that. "Oh dear," he said. "Oh dear, oh dear. Well in that case I suppose Mungo will have to wait a little longer."

He went over to give Steve his description while Longdon tapped Spalding on the shoulder.

"Which film was this one from, then?" he asked.

"*Hands of the Ripper*, Inspector," Spalding replied. "A 1971 film famous for its climax in St Paul's Cathedral. It's actually a girl who falls to her death but otherwise I'm quite surprised at how faithful Valentine managed to make his reconstruction."

Longdon failed to be impressed. "Let's stick with Valentine himself, shall we?" he said. "I don't suppose any of you journos did any detailed research on him? You didn't by any chance find out about any wives? Lovers? Sisters? Anyone else who might be the girl he had with him?"

Spalding gave him a wry grin. "It probably won't surprise you to learn that 'we journos' had a good old look into Dr Valentine's history. And no — he had one wife, now deceased, no sisters, and no illicit affairs."

"At least none who would own up to it," Longdon pointed out.

"We offered a very tidy sum to anyone who could come forward with any dirt on the doctor," said Spalding, "especially of the lurid and debauched kind, and we came up with nothing. Until he decided to go on his rampage of death he seems to have led a pretty spotless life. Cared for his patients, loyal to his staff. The bugger was probably kind to animals as well."

"He probably still is," Longdon was rubbing his chin in thought.

"And he probably still believes that some human life should be preserved — just not the kind that crosses him. Which means we could be looking for a very grateful patient, or even someone who sympathised with his story and somehow managed to find him out."

"That's a bit far-fetched, don't you think, Inspector?" Spalding shook his head. "Are you suggesting someone might have sympathised with him enough to want to commit murder? To actually take a human life?"

"I'm not sure everyone in this country would go so far as to describe your kind of journalist as human, Mr Spalding." Longdon raised an eyebrow. "And I'd suggest you don't forget that."

Spalding gave the Inspector a cold look. "Meaning what, exactly?"

"Meaning that I have been dragged back here to investigate a series of murders where even I can sympathise with the murderer," said Longdon. "Don't forget I read those newspaper articles too, and I and my staff didn't exactly come out of the whole thing unscathed. You people don't care what you write as long as it sells papers, and yet the minute your own health is threatened and your own lives are endangered, you come to us expecting to be protected by the very hands you've bitten time and time again. I can understand our Dr Valentine's motives only too well, Mr Spalding. and while I am not the most sensitive of men I certainly have a little bit of sympathy for him, something that is somewhat lacking when it comes to you and your colleagues."

Spalding, stunned at Longdon's outburst, said nothing. Now that the Inspector had stopped speaking, the gaunt silence that surrounded them seemed claustrophobic, despite the vast space in which they were standing.

"I see, Inspector," he said eventually. "I'm sorry you feel that way. I hope it isn't going to affect the investigation."

Longdon shook his head. "Just because I don't like you doesn't mean I'm going to let you get killed, Spalding, and I'm sure you realise that. Don't get me wrong — I've every intention of capturing our Dr Valentine. He got away from me once and you people made me a laughing stock. I've no intention of that happening again."

Longdon turned to see that Ronald was making for the door.

"All finished are we?" Longdon called after him. The little man quickened his pace in case he was about to be called back, but Longdon was already on his way over to Steve the artist.

"Very nice," he said as he inspected Steve's sketch. "I'm not surprised our Mr Turner-Wyatt could remember her. She shouldn't be too difficult to find." Spalding was peering over his shoulder. "I don't suppose you recognise her, do you?"

Spalding shook his head and coughed to clear his throat. "I've never seen her before," he replied. "More's the pity."

"We'll get this picture circulated," said Longdon. " See if anyone knows anything about her."

"Do you think that's wise?" said Spalding. "Surely it will simply alert Valentine to the fact that now we know what his accomplice looks like."

"I don't bloody care what Valentine knows," Longdon snapped. "The bugger's always two steps ahead of us anyway. This is the first lead we've had and while it's probably going to turn out to be part of some master plan of his I'm going to milk it for all it's worth."

"Well you'd better hurry up, Inspector," said Spalding, no longer veiling the cynicism in his voice now that Longdon had revealed what he thought of him. "After all, there are only two of us left. If the entire might of the British police force can't prevent us from being killed you deserve everything that any of my currently uninvolved colleagues end up writing about you."

"Oh we'll stop him," said Longdon. "Don't you worry about that. Right now there are three DIs on their way down to where Martin Peyton, formerly of the Daily Mail, is currently on holiday."

"And where might that be, Inspector?" Spalding asked. "Wales? Bournemouth?"

Longdon shook his head and said the name of a place that gave both of them a feeling of dread inevitability.

"Cornwall."

NINE

Penzance was a wonderful place for a holiday, Martin Peyton thought as he stretched in the midday sunshine. He should have done this ages ago. The deck chair in which he was currently sitting creaked against his weight as he put his half-empty can of lager down on the folding table beside him. The minute they had arrived at the caravan site the kids had insisted they go swimming, and so his wife Caroline had volunteered to do child supervision as long as he promised to have the caravan opened up by the time they got back. It hadn't taken long, and now Martin was enjoying a quiet beer before the inevitably noisy return of five year old Oliver and seven year old Melanie, with no doubt a damp and weary Caroline trailing behind them.

What he did not expect was for a police car to pull up and three plainclothes detectives to get out.

"Can I help you, officers?" he asked, getting to his feet and suddenly feeling rather foolish in his gaily coloured Hawaiian shirt, shorts and flip-flops.

The one who looked like a wrestler flashed an ID badge at him. "DI Derek Martinus, sir. Can you confirm that you are Mr Martin Peyton?" Martin nodded. "Of 27 Palmentry Row, Birmingham?"

"If I have to admit I live there then, yes," Martin replied with a grin. The officers did not seem amused.

Now the severe-looking woman spoke. "DI Susannah Graves," she said, with a flourish of her badge. "Can you also confirm that you are the author of the articles 'Sick Surgeon Killed His Own Kind', 'Demented Doctor Dealt Death to Nine' and — " there was a pause before this one, " — The Medical Madman and the Incompetent Inspector: How Malpractice Cost Taxpayers Thousands'?"

Peyton nodded slowly. "I did," he said. "Might I ask why any of that is important?"

The third man identified himself as DI Colin Wentworth. He had a thin face that Martin imagined probably rarely smiled, and today was no exception. "We have reason to believe your life is in danger, sir."

"What?" The journalist did his best to look properly incensed. "Who on earth would want to kill me?"

Graves raised her eyebrows. "Those newspaper headlines haven't given you a clue, then?"

"No they haven't, Miss Graves," Martin tried to look behind them to see if there was any sign of Caroline and the kids coming back. "And if you don't mind I'd appreciate you leaving before my family returns. I don't want them upset by you being here."

"With all due respect, sir," said Martinus, shifting awkwardly from foot to foot, "I think they'd find it more distressing if they came back to find you'd been skewered through the chest."

"Or crushed," added Graves.

"Or hung by the neck from a convenient tree, like the one just over there." Wentworth helpfully pointed to a big old oak towering over wooden slats that demarcated the camp's toilets.

Martin sank into his chair. "What the hell are you lot on about?"

"It's Dr Valentine, sir," said Martinus. "Over the past few days we believe he's killed a number of your colleagues, and there's a good chance you could be next."

"Ah." Martin Peyton went quiet as he stared hard at the ground. Eventually he looked up at them again. "And I suppose you've been sent down here for my protection, have you?"

"Something like that, sir," said Wentworth. "Of course, the best thing for you to do would be to come with us so we could keep you in protective custody until this is all over."

"But you know I'm going to refuse," Martin replied. "Don't you?"

"I can tell from your face, sir," said Wentworth, "even if you haven't actually said it yet."

Martin rung his hands, checked again to make sure there was no sign of his family, and then gave the officers a pleading look.

"This is my last chance with Caroline and the kids," he said. "She's threatened to leave me a couple of times now, and to take them with her. She doesn't like what I do any more than you do. In fact I've been thinking of chucking it all in and getting a nice quiet job down here working on the local paper. You know, covering church fetes and local sporting events. And I just might do that. But if she sees you people here she'll leave me for certain."

"We can't leave you alone, sir," said Graves. "We're under orders."

"And what do your orders say, exactly?"

"That we are to keep you under observation at all times," said Martinus, "and intervene if your life appears to be in any kind of danger."

"So you could keep an eye on me from a distance, then?"

None of them looked happy about that.

"But you could?" Martin looked desperate. "You could follow me anywhere you need to, watch me all the time, but keep yourselves out of the way enough that my family won't know you're there?"

"We're not exactly trained for covert operations, Mr Peyton," said Wentworth. "We're just simple coppers who want to prevent you from being strung up."

"Or stabbed," said Graves.

"Or crushed," added Martinus.

"Or dissolved in acid," said Wentworth for good measure. "You do see our problem, don't you?"

Martin nodded. He was starting to sweat now. "I do, I do, but please. You don't know how important it is that the kids don't think there's anything wrong. And Caroline too." Martin looked around nervously. "Especially Caroline."

The detectives conferred. It wasn't long before there was the sound of children's laughter from behind them. Martin jumped and Wentworth gave him a sour look.

"You have to promise us you won't do anything to endanger yourself," he said.

Martin nodded. "Of course."

"And that you won't go wandering off on your own," said Graves.

"I promise," Martin agreed.

"And whatever you do," said Martinus, "do not allow yourself to be drawn away by any kind of weird invitation, no matter how attractive a prospect it might be."

"I'm with my family," Martin said, too loudly and with a laugh so insincere it could only have been intended for the sun-tanned attractive woman behind them who was doing her best to herd her children towards the caravan.

"Darling?" Caroline's pretty face was already creased into a frown. "Who are these people?"

Martin did his best to look nonchalant, but despite years of working on a national daily he couldn't quite dispel his aura of shiftiness, especially not in front of his wife.

"They're policemen," he said, before quickly adding a "sorry" in the direction of DI Graves.

"Oh God, I warned you," Caroline said. "Any more funny business with bloody oil sheiks, or exclusive interviews with people on the run, and I told you what would happen." She called to the two children who had scampered into the caravan to change out of their moist clothes.

"It's not what you think!" Martin said, his eyes darting from her to the three detectives in the hope of some corroboration.

"Isn't it?" Caroline's eyes narrowed as she waited for one of them to say something.

"Your husband isn't in any trouble, Mrs Peyton," said Martinus eventually. "Quite the opposite, in fact. Hopefully he's helping us to prevent a murder."

Caroline gave her husband an accusing look. "Just as long as it's not his own," she said. "You won't believe how many scummy low life types he's rubbed mucky shoulders with in the past, in the hope of some bloody headline the world would probably be better off without anyway."

"I'm afraid we can't say any more," DI Graves interjected, saving everyone from digging themselves into ever-deepening holes. "But if you see us around, don't worry. It's all just a precautionary measure."

The three of them got back into the car. As they drove away Caroline turned to Martin, her eyes blazing. "Precautionary against what, might I ask?"

Martin shrugged and held out his hands. "I can't tell you," he said. "If I did I'd be in trouble."

"You're in trouble already," said Caroline. "And if you don't tell me you're going to be spending the rest of the fortnight here on your own."

"Mummy!"

"Daddy!"

The first voice was Oliver's, the second Melanie's. The couple turned to see their children standing in the doorway of the caravan. The little girl was holding a crumpled piece of paper.

"What's that you've got there, Mel?" Martin asked, desperate for any form of distraction.

The girl came forward and shyly held the paper up with one hand, while hooking the index finger of the other firmly inside her mouth.

"The scary lady gave it to us," said Oliver from behind her.

"She wasn't scary," said Caroline, in way that was probably intended to sound reassuring, but in her current state of anger it just sounded as if she was telling them off. Melanie cringed away from Mummy's outstretched hand as she gave the paper to Daddy.

Martin did a better job of smiling than Caroline had managed as he read the garish red print out loud.

"Dr Terror's Haunted Cornish Funfair," he said, at the same time taking in the array of gruesome characters that surrounded the words.

"Can we go can we go can we go can we can we can we can we?!!" Oliver came tearing out of the caravan with a battle cry and rammed straight into his father.

Martin hugged his boy and gave both his children his best funny face. It made them both giggle. "You don't want to go to a Haunted Funfair do you?" he said.

"Yes!" the two children chorused.

"But won't it be too scary for you?"

"No!"

Martin crouched down and gave them both a serious stare. "Not even if I make you go in the Haunted House...by yourselves!"

There was a pause as the children considered this. Then Melanie took Oliver's hand and said "I'll look after him."

"Yes, Melanie will look after me!" Oliver's trust in his slightly older sister's ability to protect him from danger caused both parents to gaze at him adoringly for a moment.

"Hey guys, it'll all be fine," Martin said with a glance to his wife. "Nobody's going to go on anything without one of us with you ."

"Thank you Daddy!" Melanie ran forward to give Martin a big kiss.

"We're going we're going we're going we're going!" Oliver was already charging around demonstrating how he was going to fight zombies, as Martin Peyton realised he had somehow been duped into taking his children to the fair.

The field in which Dr Terror had decided to erect his Haunted Cornish Funfair was just beyond the outskirts of the town, but that didn't seem to have harmed its business at all. In fact, on this midsummer Saturday afternoon, the place was packed. Martin found a narrow parking space in the next field along, squeezing the family's four wheel drive between a camper van and a black Audi. Martin couldn't help taking a closer look at the tiny toy voodoo doll with the needles through its heart hanging from the Audi's rear view mirror, before the relentless cries of his children urged him to follow both them and his wife in the direction of the glittering summer noise.

"Don't think I've forgotten what we were discussing," Caroline hissed as Martin dug in his pocket for his wallet. The bored-looking girl in the ticket booth ignored the bouncing children and barely registered Martin as he slid two notes across. They were all rewarded with barely-legible stamps of black ink on their hands and a sheet of tickets for the rides.

"Look at this!" said Martin as they tramped across grass that looked ready to die. "A free ride on each attraction!"

"Me me me me me me me!" With all the egotistical zeal of a five year old, Oliver had already assumed that the tickets were intended for him.

Melanie jumped up and down, trying to read the sheet as Martin walked. "Where's mine?" she whined.

"You forgot to get two sheets," Caroline spat.

"I wasn't given two sheets, was I?" Martin snapped in return. "Besides, I think I can afford rides for everyone."

"That's not the point, is it?" said his wife, determined not to let it go. "Whichever child gets the free ticket will think they're special in your eyes, and the other one's sense of self worth could be ruined!"

"Then I'll alternate who gets the tickets," Martin sighed, wishing she'd never read that child psychology book. He looked at the tickets and wondered which they should try first. The 'Zombies in the Haunted Tin Mine' sounded as if it might be a bit too scary, and something claiming to be 'Dr Blood's Coffin' would probably be a bit too much for them as well. They might find the waxworks museum boring, and these local things were never up to much, so they could give the 'Crucible of Terror' a miss. Judging by the absence of a queue outside the tent's rather scarred-looking entrance, everyone else had decided to do the same thing.

"Now you seem like a man willing to take a challenge!"

The man who had suddenly appeared in front of them seemed far too well dressed for a carnival showman. He didn't sound like one either, Martin thought.

"I'm not so sure about that," Martin said, stepping to one side.

The man mirrored his movement. "Oh I think you are, my dear sir. Allow me to introduce myself. My name is Dr Franklyn." He noticed Caroline's frown. "Not a medical doctor, my good lady, oh goodness me, no. My doctorate is in the twin disciplines of entertainment and excitement, and," he turned back to Martin now, "I do not believe for one second that you are the kind of man who would shirk a test of bravery before his entire family!"

Martin looked at his scowling wife, and then down at his two children, who were regarding their father with all the trust and adoration he didn't deserve. He remembered the words of the police officers, but this wasn't something out of the ordinary, at least not in the context of a fairground. What possible harm could come to him here?

"All right," he said, flashing Caroline a determined look. "Lead me to it."

"Why, my dear sir," said Franklyn with a gesture of his cane, "we are practically upon it."

The Peyton family looked up at the banner over the fairground ride ahead of them. "Dare You Ride 'The Reptile'?" screamed ivory-coloured letters. The first and last of each word had been embellished with blood-dripping fangs. Rather than lend the phrase a sense of spooky fun, Martin thought it all looked rather sinister. He looked down at his sheet of tickets. The free ride on The Reptile was in the bottom left hand corner.

"We only have the one ticket," he said with a shrug.

Franklyn tapped the height restriction sign. "I'm afraid the little ones aren't quite grown up enough to enjoy this one yet," he said, "and I imagine you'll be wanting your wife to look after them if you're going to take a spin?"

Martin shook his head. "In that case it's probably best if I don't bother with it at all," he said.

"Oh go on, Daddy," said Oliver. "I want to see the fangs. Rahhhhhhhh!!!!"

"What kind of a ride is it?" Melanie asked.

"Merely a waltzer of the old fashioned variety," said Franklyn, indicating the green-painted merry-go-round, "but with a few little surprises thrown in."

Martin took a closer look at the ride. The whole thing had been painted an unappetising green. Each carriage had room for one, or possibly two at a squeeze. But that wasn't the thing that bothered him.

It was the fact that each carriage was in the shape of a snake's head.

The seat was red, the scarlet plastic presumably intended to emulate the interior of the snake's gaping mouth. The moulded plastic canopy boasted a pair of glaring yellow eyes set into green-black scales. Two huge fangs descended from the canopy to touch the floor, matched only by the pair that curved upwards from the cigarette-burned linoleum to meet the roof. They were obviously the safety bars, but they looked more likely to do harm than protect.

"I suppose it'll be all right," said Martin, trying to keep the uncertainty out of his voice.

"Of course, my dear sir," Franklyn assured him.

"Why isn't there anyone else on it?" Caroline asked.

"It's only just been re-opened," was the reply. "In fact my assistant is just this moment about the ticket booth."

They all turned to see a pretty girl in a slinky emerald dress making her way into the tiny cabin at the front.

"My daughter, you know, and late again," said Franklyn with a slight trace of irritation. "She can be a great burden to me."

"Well I don't fancy going on it by myself," said Martin.

"Oh you won't, my dear chap, you won't! As you can see, there is already a queue beginning to build." They all looked behind them to see that indeed there was. "But as you've been good enough to lend me your time and attention, you get the opportunity to ride in the best seat." Franklyn indicated the chair closest to the entry gate. "Now what do you say? You won't get another chance like this all day. It's always one of our most popular rides."

"Go ON, Daddy!" Oliver was insistent. "I want to see you in the shark's mouth!"

"It's a snake, darling," Caroline patted Oliver's head. "Go on, then," she said to her husband. "We haven't seen anything suitable for the children to ride on yet, so you may as well entertain them by going on this."

With no alternative but to go along with everyone else's wishes, Martin gave a resigned nod. Dr Franklyn lifted up the snake's upper jaw to allow him to sit within the red raw lining of its mouth. Once Martin was comfortable, the fangs were brought down, and locked into place.

"Comfortable?" Franklyn asked. Martin gave him a weak smile in reply. "Good! Now we just have to wait for some more of the cars to fill, and then you'll be on your way."

Martin's family were herded back behind the safety railing as Martin watched others taking their place inside the cars. They were mostly teenagers, although there were a couple of people older than him, so he didn't feel quite as self-conscious as he might have done otherwise.

He looked around the inside of the carriage. The green paint was peeling, revealing what was probably zinc plate beneath.

Except no, it wasn't.

Martin craned his head forward and picked at a tongue of crumbling green enamel to his left. It came to pieces in his fingers. What was revealed looked odd, and certainly not what he would expect the bare bones of a fairground carriage to look like.

It almost looked like...words.

The carriage began to move off as Martin fumbled for his mobile phone. He thumbed a random button to cause the screen to light up, and then held it close to the place he had stripped the paint from.

There were words.

Tiny words.

Newsprint.

Martin felt a spasm of concern as the chamber rattled and rocked a little from side to side. He hoped they hadn't done a swift repair job on it by plugging any holes with newspaper.

The carriage rounded a corner as Martin reached out and picked more paint away. This time he revealed enough that he could read whole sentences.

His sentences.

The carriage jerked again as Martin found himself reading his own article. The last one he had written for that paper. The last headline that policewoman had quoted at him with something approaching disdain in her voice.

The carriage began to turn round.

Martin, not strapped in, reached out with both hands to either side of the carriage to brace himself.

The paint there crumbled and came away, too, revealing more newsprint, more news stories.

All his news stories.

All about the same thing.

The same man.

The carriage was starting to spin, now, faster and faster. Despite his flailing efforts to keep himself steady, Martin found himself being flung from side to side.

The first time he saw blood he thought he must have scratched his hand on a rough piece of metal.

As the carriage slowed he saw the spike that had emerged from the wall on the left. It was only a couple of inches long, but the point was sharp and diamond shaped, designed to create a wound that wouldn't heal well. But that wasn't the worst of it. The skin where the metal had penetrated was swiftly swelling and turning black, the infection or poison or whatever it was spreading over his palm.

Almost as if he had been bitten by a venomous snake.

Martin barely had time to inspect the wound further before the chamber began to spin once more. Martin pushed himself away from the penetrating metal, only to feel something pierce his back from the other side of the carriage. He pulled himself away to see another spike had appeared there as well. Burning agony shot up his spine.

Now more spikes were beginning to appear, from both sides, the back and from the roof as well. The seat on which Martin was sitting was slippery with blood. It was impossibly to tell how much because the material was the same colour as what was flowing out of him. His skin was swelling everywhere, now, the flesh turning black and mottled. He felt foam begin to bubble between his lips.

As the carriage began to spin faster and faster and Martin gave up all hope of keeping himself away from the spikes that were still appearing, all he could think of was how horrified his family would be when the jaws of what had become his tomb were finally prised apart.

TEN

The atmosphere in the incident room in Bristol was decidedly chilly.

Martinus, Graves and Wentworth had arrived back from Cornwall in the early hours of the morning. To say Longdon had been unhappy with what they had to report would have been an understatement. Now they sat with nothing to say while Longdon leaned back on his chair and stared at the map of the British Isles next to the door. A red drawing pin indicated the site of each murder, and a piece of red wool led from each pin to a mini reproduction of the poster for the corresponding Hammer film.

There were now six of them.

"That wall looks more like an advert for a horror film festival than a murder investigation," Longdon growled. He took a gulp of coffee so strong that even he found himself coughing at the bitterness of it. He looked at his three colleagues. "How the hell could the three of you have let Peyton out of your sight?"

"We didn't, sir," said Martinus under his breath.

"What?!" Longdon bellowed, causing the bigger man to physically recoil.

"What he means, sir," said Graves, "is that we were there all the time. In fact we were practically standing behind his family while the ride was going. We couldn't possibly have known that — "

"Of course you could!" Longdon tipped forward on his chair and put the coffee cup on the table. He got up, thrust his hands into his pockets, and began to pace before them. "This is Valentine, remember? A man who seems to be able to do anything, from catapulting someone off a cliff to rigging up an entire fairground to suit his demented purpose." He placed his palms flat on the table and glared at them. "Did none of you recognise him?"

They all shook their heads.

"He didn't look anything like the pictures we were given," said Graves. "But he was very well spoken."

"And what about the girl?" Longdon pointed to the sketch Steve the artist had made at St Paul's. A portrait-sized reproduction was now stuck on the wall next to the Hammer posters.

"Yes sir," said Wentworth. "That was definitely her. But with respect, sir, that picture didn't get transmitted to us until after Mr Peyton's demise, so there's no way we could have identified her."

"I know, I know," Longdon waved his hand in a dismissive gesture. "It just means we've only one more chance to stop him."

"And you better had, Inspector," said Spalding from next to the water cooler. "Because for your information I've already written a nice little exposé about this investigation so far. And if anything happens to me, my lawyers have instructions to deliver it to the highest bidder."

Graves gave Spalding a weary glance. "Why should you be bothered about how much money it sells for if you're dead?" she said.

"Because," said the journalist, "the more it sells for, the more the newspaper concerned will make sure that the story isn't just plastered all over the front page for several incisive, thought-provoking issues, it'll make sure the thing is shouted from the rooftops so everyone knows how incompetent you all are."

"I'll provoke your thoughts in a minute, Mr Spalding," said Longdon. "And I can assure you it won't be with a newspaper."

"Shouldn't you be hard at work trying to apprehend Valentine rather than sitting here thinking up new ways of insulting me?" said Spalding, looking round the room. "In fact, shouldn't all of you?" Before he could say anything else, the reporter grimaced and got carefully to his feet. "If you'll excuse me," he said, clutching his stomach, "I think all these events are beginning to get to me." He began to walk awkwardly towards the door. "By the time I come back I hope you'll have thought of something else to do other than just sit here trading insults and apologies."

Once the door had closed Martinus spoke up.

"Do we have to keep him with us all the time, sir?" he asked. "He's starting to get on my nerves."

The others nodded as Longdon shook his head. "We have to have him under maximum police protection," he said. "You've all seen how skilful Valentine is at murdering people under our very noses. In fact for all we know he could be hiding in the cubicle outside preparing to abduct Spalding as we speak."

The room went very quiet at that. The silence was only broken by the distant sound of a toilet being flushed.

"What are we going to do, sir?" said Graves. 'We're still without any useful leads at all. There have been no identifications of that girl, and we've made no progress working out where Valentine might be based."

Longdon regarded the map. "You're right there," he said. "I was hoping the murders might have been centred around one particular area of the country, but they're scattered all over the place."

"What about where he used to live?" said Wentworth.

"You mean the former residence of 'Dr Richard Patterson', the name he hid behind the first time around?" replied Longdon. "That was one of the first things I had checked out. It was bought for a song at an auction held a couple of months after it was clear Valentine wasn't coming back, and if he was it would be to a nice cosy prison cell rather than his mansion in North Somerset."

"Who bought it, sir?" asked Graves.

Longdon looked around him, and then lifted a bulging file off the floor. "I made a note of it in here somewhere," he said, flicking through papers before selecting a tissue-thin yellow sheet. "It would seem the property was sold to an elderly widow by the name of Mrs E Brandt."

"And that's not a Hammer film character, is it?" Graves was already typing the name into a search engine on her tablet.

"I don't think Valentine would do anything quite so obvious," said Longdon. "It's been checked but it wouldn't hurt for you to take another look." Graves was already shaking her head. "There are too many entries for Brandt on IMDB," she said. "It could take ages to go through them all."

"Spalding might know," Martinus piped up.

"He might at that." Longdon looked over to the door. "Where the hell is he anyway?"

"Perhaps we should go and check?" Wentworth was already on his feet.

With Longdon in the lead, the four of them made their way down the corridor outside as quietly as possible. They halted when they came to a white door on the left. A black outline indicated it was the gents' toilet.

The door was closed.

Longdon knocked twice, rapid and loud, before speaking even more loudly. "Are you all right in there, Mr Spalding?"

There was no reply.

Longdon tried the door handle. It was locked. He took a step back and aimed his shoulder at the plywood.

"Shouldn't you try once more?" asked Martinus as the door splintered inward.

"Mr Spalding, are you in here?" Longdon bellowed to the empty toilet cubicle before them. He stepped inside and looked around.

"Maybe he went to get something to eat," said Wentworth.

"I don't think so." Longdon was reaching above him to take down a gold-bordered invitation card that had been wedged above the inside of the lintel. "It would appear our Dr Valentine has left us a message this time."

The four of them stared at the seven words that had been written on the card in Prussian blue ink:

At home this evening. Guests are welcome.

ELEVEN

The four police officers arrived at Valentine's Somerset mansion just after sunset. The Victorian country house was in darkness as they got out of the car.

"Are you sure this is where Valentine meant, sir?" Martinus was searching the mullioned windows for a trace of light, but none was forthcoming.

"Of course I am," said Longdon, making sure his special issue firearm was loaded. He had insisted the others be armed as well, and they all looked equally uncomfortable about the possible need for them to wield guns.

"I really don't think he's going to attack us, sir," Graves argued. "And anything he has in store for Spalding is bound to take the form of some complex creation that guns will be useless against."

"They might just convince him to stop whatever he's doing, though," Longdon replied with a snarl. "We're going in with guns, and that's an end to it."

Wentworth turned up the collar of his jacket against the cold breeze that had sprung up. "How can you be so certain this is where he's holding Spalding, sir?" he asked.

"A couple of reasons." Longdon tried the cast iron handle of the front door. It swung open with a creak. "First, if he wanted us to be his guests for the evening then the venue couldn't be that far from Bristol. Second, this is the most likely place for him to want to meet, especially as it probably appeals to his sense of humour to have a final face-off in the place where I met him before. But finally, and the one that really clinches it, the name 'Mrs E Brandt' is in a Hammer Horror film after all. She's a minor character in something called *Frankenstein Must Be Destroyed*, a film that also happens to feature an isolated country house."

"What happens in the film?" asked Wentworth with yet another shiver.

"Oh, apparently Frankenstein saws some chap's head open to try and swap his brain with someone else, but it all goes a bit wrong." Longdon shone his torch into the hallway. "Still," he said, looking behind him at Wentworth, "the house burns to the ground at the end, so if that happens tonight at least it'll warm you up a bit. Right now, though, I'd appreciate it if you would kindly cover my back."

Wentworth followed Longdon into the building, while Martinus and Graves were given instructions to go round the back of the house and find another way in "Just in case we end up strung up by the staircase," Longdon said, with little trace of amusement in his tone. "If you hear us screaming, you come running. Understand?"

Graves and Martinus nodded, drew their weapons, and went off to circumvent the house from the right.

"What's it like being back here, sir?" Wentworth whispered as Longdon flicked a nearby light switch.

"Bloody electricity must have been disconnected," said Longdon as he swiped at the switch once more. The house stayed dark. "Bloody disconcerting is what it is, son," he said, answering

Wentworth's question. "Bloody disconcerting." He shone his torch up the broad staircase on the left. "Valentine kept his mummified daughter upstairs," he said. "My colleague Jenny Newham found her body propped in front of a television set showing old Vincent Price films over and over."

Wentworth nodded. "I remember reading about it," he said, looking around the entry hall. "Was the place as bare as this when you were here?"

Longdon shook his head as they inspected the oak-panelled walls. "There were all sorts of trophies and paintings," he said. "But it looks as if they all got sold off in the auction." He indicated a door to his right. "If I remember correctly," he said, "in here was what he liked to call the drawing room."

This door creaked as well, and utter blackness lay beyond it. Unsurprisingly, the light switch for the lounge also failed to work.

"You'd think he'd have made things a bit more welcoming," said Longdon, as he shone his torch ahead of him.

"Perhaps we've got it wrong," whispered Wentworth from behind him. "Perhaps he didn't mean this place after all."

"Rubbish!" Longdon was still certain. "Besides, if I'm wrong, where's Mrs so-called Brandt? Why hasn't she furnished this place rather than leaving it like a tomb after the grave-robbers have been in?"

"You're starting to sound like those old films, sir," said Wentworth with a nervous chuckle.

"I certainly feel as if I'm living in one of them sometimes," Longdon replied.

Then all the lights came on.

The two men shielded their eyes against the harsh glare as, from the speakers that had been positioned all around the room, well-spoken tones that were familiar to Longdon began to address them.

"Good evening, gentlemen," said Valentine. "And in particular, may I say how pleasant it is to see you again, Inspector Longdon. I must confess I rather hoped we had not seen the last of each other. How strange to be talking to you once again within the walls of my old home."

Longdon took his hand from his face as the lights dimmed a little to reveal their source — four floodlights set up on gantries positioned to the left and right of the far side of the room.

"Is that better?" Valentine said. "I must apologise. It was not my intention to dazzle you to such an extent. At least, not with mere stage lights."

"As opposed to your searing intellectual genius?" Longdon shouted into the void above them created by the glare. "I'm not sure what you're hoping to prove, Valentine, but my advice is for you to give up now. The house is surrounded."

There was a chuckle at that. "I hope you'll forgive me, Inspector," he said, "but I believe I've heard that line somewhere before. And it didn't do you or your sergeant much good last time, did it? Now forget about barking whatever you believe will pass for your next pithy witticism and please pay attention to what, or rather who, is in front of you."

Longdon followed Wentworth's horrified gaze to the man sitting in between the spotlights at the far end of the room. For a moment he almost didn't recognise that it was Spalding. This was partly because "sitting" wasn't an entirely accurate way of describing how the man had been secured there. His wrists and ankles had been attached to the stout metal supports by thick clasps. Another broad band of shining steel ran around his waist to keep him upright. But the most intricate method of restraint had been reserved for Spalding's head and neck. A stout leather brace around his throat prevented him from lowering or raising his chin. The cushioned rubber ends of rigid steel supports had been placed tight up against each cheek, so any movement of the head from side to side was an impossibility.

But the thing Longdon was most concerned about was the drill that had been placed perpendicular to the apex of Spalding's shaved skull. There was a gap of about three inches between the pointed tip of the heavy drill bit, and Spalding's recently scraped scalp, which still bore tiny traces of fresh blood where the razor had nicked the skin.

"I'm looking, Valentine," said Longdon. "What am I supposed to do now?"

"Oh nothing, Inspector," said the voice. "By which I mean if you do anything at all, even move, in fact especially move, it will spell the downfall for poor old Mr Spalding."

"What do you mean?" Longdon was about to take a step back when Wentworth stopped him and pointed at the floor.

Which was now laced with a spiderweb of fine metal strands that glinted in the glare of the spotlights. But only if you looked at them at just the right angle.

"Any movement of the fibres will start the drill," said Valentine. "And the more fibres that are broken, the faster the drill will spin."

"What bloody Hammer film is that in, then?" said Longdon, now shouting at the ceiling again.

"It's not," said Valentine. "But the man before you awaiting some rather blunt Victorian-style brain surgery is certainly from one. I'm sure I don't have to help you with it, Inspector. It's exactly what you're thinking."

"What?" Longdon looked confused and almost took a step forward before his colleague stopped him again.

"Frankenstein Must Be Destroyed." The muffled words from between Spalding's compressed lips were just sufficiently intelligible, even to the ears of the gruesome scene's offstage creator, who responded with another low chuckle.

"Indeed!" Valentine said. "But I very much suspect it is I whom Inspector Longdon would like to see destroyed at this very moment."

"You'd be bloody right about that," Longdon growled. He lifted a foot, one of the wires went twang, and the drill started turning.

"Oh dear, Inspector," said Valentine. "I do believe you've put Mr Spalding one step closer to a nasty death. A very nasty death indeed."

"This isn't a very Hammer way to end it all, Valentine," said Longdon. "I'd have thought you'd want to finish this little series of murders with more than a few pieces of clanking metal."

"Oh, this is not the end, Inspector," came the reply. "Not for you, and certainly not for me. But I wanted to see you tonight to tell you that by now you should hopefully have worked out where our final showdown should be. If not, then I'll ask you to think once again about Mr Peyton's death. If that doesn't help, then go back to your source material. For now, however, I agree with you. This scene isn't quite typical of the Hammer horrors I have been taking such pains to try and reproduce. I'm sure you know what's missing, as well."

There was the sound of an electrical circuit being completed, and the curtains to the left of the window burst into flame.

"Enjoy trying to save yourselves, Inspector," Valentine was laughing now. "To say nothing of our journalist friend. And if you do make it out of here alive, have fun working out where to come looking for me."

As Spalding struggled against the steel restraints the flames spread along the floor and made contact with the cables running up to the left bank of floodlights. There was a hiss as the plastic insulation melted, and then a loud bang from the left lighting gantry. Tiny fragments of burning glass and metal peppered Spalding, making his struggles all the more frantic.

"You can't, sir!" screamed Wentworth as Longdon made to lunge forward. Another metal thread broke and the drill began to descend towards Spalding's skull.

"Well, what are we supposed to do?" Longdon shouted in return. "Just stand here and watch him die?"

There was no response from above them. Valentine was already making good his escape.

"That's obviously what we are bloody well are supposed to do," Longdon added, shielding his brow from the heat with his left arm while he stared at the intricate criss-cross pattern of metal, now glowing orange from the reflected flames. His concentration was interrupted by a crash from ahead of him.

The window panes to the right had exploded inward, and the faces of Graves and Martinus were now poking through.

"Don't come in here!" Longdon shouted. "You'll kill him!"

But it was already too late. The flames, drawn towards the fresh air, ignited the right hand lighting gantry. As Spalding continued to pull helplessly at his bonds, the lights exploded and the metal framework fell forwards, straight into the mesh of tripwires.

The moment he saw where the gantry was headed, Longdon lunged forward. But by the time he got there, the drill was firmly lodged in Spalding's skull. Spalding, meanwhile, had ceased to care.

TWELVE

"He said I would know where it would all end."

Longdon stared at the map. The faces of seven dead journalists stared back, their photographs pinned next to the posters for the movies that had inspired their deaths.

"It has ended, hasn't it?" Martinus was being even more tentative than usual, even though Longdon seemed to have lost his fire since Spalding's death the night before. "I mean, there's no-one else for Valentine to kill."

Longdon ran a weary hand over his face. "I know that," he said, "in the same way I know that if our good doctor hinted that he isn't finished, then he isn't finished."

DI Graves handed him a fresh cup of coffee. "Sir." She was having a hard time finding words this evening as well. "Have you considered that if you do manage to work out where he wants to you go that it might be..."

"...a trap?" Longdon regarded her with bleary eyes. "It's all I have been thinking about, DI Graves, believe you me."

The door creaked open and Wentworth pushed his way in, holding a cardboard box out in front of him. He dropped it onto a nearby table.

"Those are all the Hammer films I could get hold of on DVD," he said with a sigh. "I had no idea there were so many of them."

"Christ, neither did I." Longdon looked at the widescreen television that had been set up in the far corner. From his expression, watching anything on it was the last thing he wanted to do.

"Okay," he said eventually, getting to his feet. "We'll do it in shifts. Eight hours each, and in pairs in case one of us misses anything." He rummaged in the box and pulled out a disc. "I feel a bit like I'm running the lucky dip at the local fair," he said. His colleagues stayed quiet. "Yes you're quite right," he added. "That wasn't funny at all." He looked at the garish picture of a woman with snake's eyes and fangs poised to leap off the cover. "He said to think about the death of Martin Peyton, so who fancies watching *The Reptile* with me?"

Martinus jerked a thumb towards the map. "Is there any point, sir? He's already used that for a murder."

Longdon put a hand on his shoulder. "All the more reason for watching it and paying close attention then, DI Martinus," he said, "and thank you for volunteering. Valentine said we'd know where it would end so maybe the clue is in one of the films he's already used as inspiration. We should be able to get through at least five of them before Graves and Wentworth take over."

Longdon urged the other two out the door, with instructions that they were to "read a book, get pissed, take sleeping tablets, whatever" as long as they got some sleep.

"I'll expect you back here at 7am sharp," he said. "And if DI Martinus and I have nodded off, you'll have the pleasure of our company as we watch what we've missed again."

Once Graves and Wentworth had gone, Longdon scraped two chairs into place. "Come on then, detective!" he said when he saw Martinus hesitate. "I'm afraid we haven't got a sofa we can cuddle up on, so it's going to have to be the Avon & Somerset

Constabulary's finest moulded plastic for our viewing pleasure. At least it'll keep you awake."

Martinus gave a shrug and took the chair on the left as Longdon loaded The Reptile into the machine and pressed 'play'. Just over ninety minutes later, the crashing music that heralded the titles of *Dracula Has Risen From the Grave* served to wake them up. *Blood From the Mummy's Tomb*, however, had them both nodding off in front of the flickering screen. As the end credits rolled on Valerie Leon's bandaged form reaching out for help, Longdon got up and switched the lights on.

"What's the time?" he asked.

Martinus looked at his watch. "3.45am, sir." He yawned. "Which one do you want to watch next?"

"Bloody none of them." Longdon shook his head in exasperation and looked at the notes he had been taking. "None of the films we've watched have had anything in common, except that the villain dies in the end."

Martinus still had his eyes half closed against the brightness of the fluorescent lighting. "Could that be what Valentine means, sir? That he's going to perform some kind of flamboyant act of suicide?"

Longdon shook his head. "That's not his style," he replied. He punched the carton of DVDs. "I'm convinced it's got something to do with these buggers."

Martinus rubbed his eyes but still couldn't open them more than a crack. "Perhaps we're barking up the wrong tree?" he said. "Maybe we need to watch some that Valentine hasn't tried to recreate yet?"

Longdon nodded. "You might be right," he said. He picked a film at random and held it up. "How about *Slave Girls*?" he said with a tired smile.

Martinus returned his grin. "Could be just the ticket for this time of the morning, sir," he said.

Longdon was already studying the synopsis. "Apparently this one's set in the jungle," he said. "So unless Dr Valentine plans on carting us all off to the back of beyond, I think we can safely give it a miss." He tossed it into the corner. A minute later *The Viking Queen* followed it, as did *The Pirates of Blood River*. "We're not going to Hong Kong either," said Longdon, as he put T*he Legend of the Seven Golden Vampires* with the others.

Next was *Plague of the Zombies* which, no matter how hard he tried to find a reason for it, Longdon couldn't reject. Into the DVD player it went and Crash Bang Boom went the opening title music.

"At least they do their best to wake you up at the start of these things," said Martinus as he did his best to sit a little more upright.

"Probably to get all those 1960s kids to sit down, shut up and watch," said Longdon, taking his seat.

They were about fifteen minutes in when Martinus tapped Longdon on the shoulder.

"We've seen all this before," he said.

Longdon rubbed his eyes. "No we haven't," the inspector replied. "I made sure to put the ones we've seen on a separate pile."

Martinus shook his head. "I don't mean that, sir. I mean we've seen this village before. In that first film we watched." Now there was a scene of the place where the villain lived. "And that house." Martinus was pointing now. "That house was in the other one as well."

"Good work, detective," said Longdon, getting out a notepad. "Maybe we are onto something after all."

The old tin mine was burning and the credits were rolling as Longdon levered himself off his seat and over to an adjacent computer terminal. With weary fingers he typed in a search for the locations of the two films.

"All shot on the same sets, apparently," he said as he peered at the screen. "And the house is somewhere called Oakley Court." He typed that in too. "It's certainly been used in a few films over the years. And it was at the end of *The Reptile.* Could that be what Valentine meant?"

There was a snoring from the other side of the room. Longdon looked at the clock. That was probably enough for one night, anyway. On a hunch he typed in 'Oakley Court events', added the month, and hit return. There were the usual wine tastings and musical tributes, and no doubt on the weekends there would be a few weddings as well. In fact something called the 'Wedded Bliss' organisation was having a conference there in five days' time. Longdon scrolled down to the relevant section and read it more closely. According to the information posted, the head of the agency, a 'Very Reverend Dr Bliss' would be revealing to select members of the press how he had founded the organisation and allowed for so many to meet with "that for which they were always intended".

"That's far too bloody fishy," said Longdon to himself. He typed in "Dr Bliss" and was rewarded with a picture of the actor Peter Cushing in clerical garb.

"From the film *Captain Clegg,*" Longdon read. "Otherwise known as *Night Creatures* and made in 1961 by..." Longdon was off his chair and shaking Martinus awake in a second.

"Up you get," he said, his eyes burning with the intensity of a zealot. "We've got a lot of work to do when the others get here."

"What?" Martinus almost fell off his chair as he struggled to wake. "Have you found something?"

Longdon nodded. "Too bloody right I have, and I have to say I'm more than a little fed up with being one step behind all the time." He pointed at the box of DVDs. "We're going to beat Valentine at his own game."

THIRTEEN

"They're ready."

Christina turned away from peeking through the crack in the heavy curtains. Beyond them lay the room in which the more than thirty guests had been assembled.

Valentine checked his reflection and picked up his black cloak.

"If you're debating whether or not to wear it," she said, "you should. They're going to want to take photographs."

Valentine nodded and shrugged it on over his black suit. "It's only appropriate, really," he said. "And I would hate to disappoint my public."

He seemed ready to go. Just as he was about to step through into the other room Christina stopped him.

"Are you sure this is what you want to do?" she said.

Valentine nodded. "If my story must be told, I would rather it was I who did the telling," he said. "Otherwise the same thing will just happen all over again, and we both have better things to do with our lives than spend them killing journalists." He took her hand in his own. "Is everything prepared?"

Christina nodded.

He looked her in the eye. "You don't have to do this with me, you know. I'm grateful to you for having come this far. I would understand if you wished to leave at this point and continue with your own life."

Christina returned his look. "This has become my life," she said, "and whether or not what we have done is for the good, I know that if I had not met you my life would have been nowhere near as worth living. I thank you for that."

Valentine smiled. "I imagine I'm never going to learn exactly why I found you in the state you were in all those months ago," he said.

"Maybe sometime," the girl replied. "But not now. Now it's time to stop all this sentimental nonsense." A mischievous gleam appeared in her eye. "You have an audience awaiting you, doctor, an audience keen to hear from the lips of Dr Valentine himself his quite remarkable story."

"Indeed." Valentine smiled. "And provided our Inspector Longdon has done his homework, this should provide a most satisfying climax to it all." He reached for the curtain, and drew it aside with a flourish.

The room had been arranged so that Valentine would enter from the back. As he strode down the central aisle the assembled individuals quietened, and by the time he had reached the lectern at the front the room was silent. He gripped either side of the polished wood, took a deep breath, and began to address them.

"Ladies and gentlemen," he said. "May I first of all thank each and every one of you for coming here today. I'm sure you will agree with me that Oakley Court Hotel is one of the most pleasant venues one could wish for in which to hold what is essentially a press conference."

There were murmurs of agreement at this.

"Sad to say," Valentine continued, "I believe the owners are thinking of selling it, and that would be a great shame. However, today they have done me the gracious gesture of allowing me to hire the entire main building. Just to ensure that we are not disturbed." He gestured to his right. Through the French windows the nearby river glittered through the net curtains. "So let us enjoy the peaceful atmosphere of this place while we can," he said. "The grounds are beautiful, and the Thames has never looked so inviting. In fact I may take a little trip on it later on myself."

There were a few chuckles at that as the atmosphere in the room began to relax.

"But now to business." Valentine looked out over the room, checking the time on the heavy clock hanging on the back wall as he did so. "I have no doubt that the police will be here soon, and I want you members of the press to hear my story before they arrive. You are journalists I have specially selected and whom I trust to report the account I am about to give you accurately and faithfully. I am sure you will not let me down."

There was a flurry of opening of notebooks and switching on of recording devices. Then the room went quiet again.

"I suppose the best place to start would be in Bristol, two years ago," said Valentine. "I had just managed to drag the body of Andrew Wells, Consultant in Accident and Emergency, to the Clifton Suspension Bridge. I had debated whether or not to dress him in the gorilla suit when I got there, but eventually decided it would be better if I encouraged him to put it on himself before I knocked him out."

Valentine was about to continue when a voice stopped him.

"That's enough, Dr Valentine."

DCI Jeffrey Longdon appeared from between the curtains at

the back. He pointed a revolver at the man who had just stopped speaking. "If you'd be kind enough to come quietly with me, sir. We don't want a scene, now do we?"

Instead of looking upset Valentine gave the policeman a broad grin. "Why Inspector! How lovely to see you! Even if it is a little before time. Did your mother never tell you that punctuality is the politeness of princes?"

Longdon was unfazed. "No sir, she was too busy showing me how to put the boot in the groin of the kids who were trying to bully me at school."

Valentine raised his eyebrows. "Really?"

"No," came the reply. "Now, are you going to come quietly or not?"

The doctor raised his arms. "But I can't possibly leave now, Inspector," he said. "Not with all the press here. They're waiting to hear my story, you see."

"Your story?"

Valentine nodded.

"You mean the one about how you've just killed seven of them in the style of the deaths in Hammer horror films?"

"I was certainly going to touch on it, Inspector," said Valentine. "Along with how I was sorely misrepresented by those particular individuals."

"Sorely misrepresented in how you killed all those doctors before you went and killed all those journalists, you mean?" Longdon was edging forward.

"Well, if you must put it so crudely, Inspector, yes."

Longdon was halfway down the aisle now. "And might it not have occurred to you, Dr Edward Valentine, that any journalist invited to a press conference like this might decide to do something other than accept their invitation? That they might instead run a country mile in the opposite direction, possibly informing the police of their intentions as they did so?"

"That thought had crossed my mind, Inspector." Valentine was moving back from the lectern now.

Longdon kept his gun trained on him. "Tell me," Longdon said, "how much research did you do before you started killing all those reporters?"

"What do you mean, research?" Valentine was against the back wall now, and there was nowhere for him to go.

"I mean," said Longdon as he approached the lectern, "how many Hammer films did you watch?"

Valentine chuckled. "Since you asked, Inspector, most of them. I rather hope that you have since done the same."

Longdon nodded. "Oh I have, sir, I have. Even stuff like *Straight On Till Morning*."

Valentine wrinkled his nose. "A pretentious thriller written by someone with art house aspirations, but lacking the talent to achieve them."

"I wouldn't know, sir," Longdon replied. "I fell asleep during that one. I stayed awake during the others, though. The old black and white psycho thrillers for example. There were some classics amongst that lot."

Valentine smiled. "Ah, yes," he said. "*Scream of Fear, Paranoiac...*"

"...and *Nightmare*." Longdon narrowed his eyes. "Do you remember the plot of *Nightmare*, sir?"

"One of many in which people try to drive a young lady mad," said Valentine. "Not especially memorable."

"Perhaps not, sir," said Longdon. "Although the way in which they tried to drive her mad did fascinate me. It's actually someone with a mask on, isn't it? A very realistic-looking mask."

Longdon raised his left hand, and as one the collected members of the press removed their remarkably life-like masks to reveal thirty members of the Metropolitan police force's finest.

Longdon gave Valentine a steely look.

"You are surrounded, sir," he said. "I suggest you give yourself up. I do hope, however, that you appreciate our little gesture to your own modus operandi."

Valentine was smiling now as he edged to the corner of the room. "Indeed I do, Inspector," he said, "just as I hope you will appreciate this."

Valentine unhooked the stout rope he had arrived at. Immediately a heavy net fell from the ceiling, trapping the police officers.

"From *Curse of the Mummy's Tomb*, Inspector," Valentine said as he ran for the exit.

Longdon swore and gave chase.

Valentine crashed through the lounge, leaping over chairs and avoiding tables. Police officers had been stationed at the main entrance and so Valentine swerved to the left and ran up the main staircase, taking the steps two at a time, his cloak billowing out behind him.

Longdon was in hot pursuit. He stopped the officers as they made to follow.

"He can't go anywhere," he shouted back to them as he ran up the stairs. "Just make sure all the exits are covered, and instruct back up teams two, three and four to do exactly what I told them."

Longdon caught up with Valentine on the first floor landing.

It ran the length of the building. Longdon was at the near end, Valentine at the far.

"Very impressive, Inspector," said Valentine, panting a little. "You know, I was rather hoping for something like this. A more suitable ending to our little tale than you carting me off in the back of a police car."

"Oh I intend to do that too, sir," said Longdon, glancing behind him at the floor-length curtains that had been drawn across the first floor windows. "But first of all I intend to do this."

With that Longdon charged towards the curtains, and pulled them down.

Blinding white light filled the landing from the bank of floodlights that had been erected behind the glass.

Valentine shielded his eyes and took a step back, almost tripping over his cloak as he did so. Just as Longdon was almost upon him Valentine grabbed a heavy candelabra and heaved it in Longdon's direction. The policeman ducked just in time, and when he looked up again Valentine was taking the next flight of stairs.

Longdon arrived on the second floor just in time to see Valentine disappear through a door marked 'Staff Only'. It led to a poorly lit flight of concrete steps, again leading upward. Longdon clattered after Valentine as the doctor opened a service door at the top that led onto the roof.

Despite the sunshine there was a distinct chill to the air as Longdon pursued Valentine past chimneys and over ventilation ducts. Finally, there was nowhere to run.

"Come on, Valentine," said a breathless Longdon as his quarry edged toward the end of the building. "You've had your fun. It's time for this particular story to end."

"What?" Valentine looked disappointed. "Don't you have

anything else, lurking out there in the grounds, Inspector? A horde of bats at your command to destroy me? A strategically placed windmill whose shadow will somehow overcome me? Aren't you even going to just try and bonk me on the head with a rock?" He looked over the edge of the building to the lawns below and frowned. The grounds were covered with mist.

"Fog canisters," said Longdon. "I thought you'd appreciate that. Of course it means even if you did make your way down you wouldn't have a hope of finding your way out of here. All my men down there are wearing gas masks. Gets in the throat, you see. Makes you cough and then probably makes you cry, too — as good as any tear gas."

Valentine nodded. As he moved slightly to the left he raised his hands and applauded. "Excellent, Inspector. I have to say I'm actually touched that you went to all this trouble."

"You've killed sixteen people, Valentine. Let me assure you that it's worth all the trouble and expense."

Valentine looked over again.

"Only if you catch me, Inspector," he said, with a grin. "It looks like it's almost as windy down there as up here. It shouldn't be too long before all your tear gas is blown away."

"There's still nowhere for you to go, Valentine." Longdon took a step forward and wielded his revolver. "I suggest you give up now. I won't hesitate to use this if I have to."

Valentine look horrified. "You wouldn't shoot a man in cold blood, would you, Inspector?"

Longdon aimed the pistol at Valentine's left leg. "You are a highly dangerous criminal, sir. All I would be doing is incapacitating you in order to make an arrest."

Valentine seemed to give that some consideration. "I suppose you have a point there, Inspector," he said. "In which case all there remains for me to say is that I really have had the most tremendous time here, and that I must thank you for all the effort you have gone to. But now it's time for me to bid you farewell."

Dr Edward Valentine raised his right hand, smiled, waved, and took a step backwards.

Straight off the building.

"Oh, shit." Longdon peered over the edge to see, through the thinning fog, the crumpled body of Valentine on the grass below.

A female police officer was already running towards him.

"Keep your distance!" Longdon shouted down. "And don't let him out of your sight!" He took out his radio to speak to Martinus. "Get an ambulance here pronto," he said, "and make sure it really is one."

"What do you mean, sir?" said the voice on the other end.

"I mean," said Longdon as he made his way back across the roof, "make sure they've got ID and that the driver is who they say they are. I don't care how many pieces Valentine might be in at the moment, he's not getting away from us this time."

By the time Longdon had made it to the front of the hotel he could already hear sirens.

"That's a bit bloody early," he said to himself, as he rounded the building to where Valentine had fallen.

The body was gone.

Wentworth, Graves and Martinus were still staring in disbelief at the spot. Martinus was on his radio to the police cars that were already in the process of cordoning off the area.

"Don't tell me," said Longdon as he approached, "you didn't check the ambulance ID."

"The ambulance hasn't got here yet," said Wentworth. "And by the time we did he'd gone."

Longdon looked at the soft Valentine-shaped depression in the grass. "What about the officer who was first on the scene?" he asked.

Graves gave him a querulous look. "We were the first on the scene, sir," she said.

Longdon shook his head. "No, no, no," he said. "There was another officer, a girl, who came running across as soon as Valentine fell. About medium height, dark hair, wearing a uniform."

Wentworth looked at his colleagues, who both gave him the same embarrassed look. "We haven't got any uniformed officers on this on, sir. They're all plainclothes."

Behind Longdon, on the Thames, a cortege of a funeral barge and two accompanying black boats was slowly making its way past the building. Meanwhile he was kicking at the ground in frustration.

"I cannot bloody believe he's got away again," he said, looking for something, or someone, to punch.

"Sir, that ground doesn't look right."

Longdon looked down to the patch of ground at which Martinus was pointing. The patch where Valentine had fallen. The patch he had just kicked.

The patch that had broken away a little, revealing the cushioned surface beneath.

Longdon crouched down and tore at the corner of the artificial grass. Then he prodded a finger into what was under it. "Sponge," he said, getting to his feet. "Bloody sponge." He looked at the others. "He knew. Valentine knew. All the time I thought we had the upper hand, that we'd managed to surprise him, and that bastard knew what we were doing every step of the way. Well, I hope his bloody bruises don't heal for a month."

"There's something else there as well, sir." Graves crouched down and pushed the green plastic cover out of the way. In the far corner was something white. She plucked it out and handed it to Longdon.

"Probably a farewell note," said Longdon as he began to unfold it. "Have you made sure all the road blocks are in place?"

Martinus nodded as Longdon read what was on the note. "All being sorted now sir," he replied. "Don't worry — he won't get far."

The funeral barge was beginning to disappear around a bend in the river as Longdon's face turned purple.

"What's the matter, sir?" asked Wentworth.

"What does it say?" asked Graves.

Longdon showed them what was written on the paper.

Don't Look Now, Inspector

As the four of them turned to face the river, the air was suddenly filled with music. Fireworks erupted from the front of the cortege as a dark figure emerged from the funeral barge, stood on the deck, and waved at them.

"Shall I send the men after him, sir?," said Martinus.

"No," said Longdon resignedly. "He's probably got a private jet waiting round the corner to fly him somewhere far, far away."

"Maybe it's not him, sir," said Graves, "and if it is, at least he won't be coming back."

That did little to lighten her DCI's mood. He raised a hand and pointed in the direction of the now vanished cortege.

"That's Valentine, all right," he said. "And he always comes back."

Longdon later put it down to his imagination, but right then he was sure that behind all the noise and the music and the showmanship, he could also detect the faintest sound of laughter.

THE END

THE HAMMER FILMS OF DR VALENTINE

If you have just finished The Hammer of Dr Valentine (and what are you doing here if you haven't? Go back and read the book now. You'll enjoy both it, and this bit, more if you do) I'm sure you'll appreciate that, amongst other things, it's a love letter to Hammer Films, a company that produced so many memorable and entertaining pictures that helped to make my childhood a lot more special than it would have been otherwise.

At the end of the special edition of The Nine Deaths of Dr Valentine, there was an appendix that provided my thoughts on the films referenced in the text, along with the usual collection of autobiographical reminiscences that I like to include at the end of my books. What follows, therefore, is not intended as a critical analysis of some of my favourite Hammer films. Rather, it is merely meant to provide an insight into the creative process that resulted in the book you now hold in your hands. As well as that, I hope it provides you with a window onto the life of a ten year old boy who, having discovered the treasure trove of fantasy that was British horror cinema, has remained spellbound and entertained by it ever since. It's impossible for me to describe just how important the films of Hammer were to me when I was growing up (and the films of Amicus, Tigon, Titan, Glendale and all the other companies that existed at the time, even it was only to produce one or two movies before vanishing) but I hope the following notes give you, the reader, some idea.

DRACULA HAS RISEN FROM THE GRAVE (1968)

This must have been one of the first Hammer films I ever saw — in ATV's 'Christopher Lee — Prince of Menace' Friday night film season back in the late 1970s. It's the third of the Draculas to star Christopher Lee, and features all kinds of things guaranteed to please thrill-hungry late 1960s audiences. Apart from the climactic impaling that inspires Dr Valentine in this story, my favourite moment has to be the apparently heretical scene where Dracula, having been staked, proceeds to wrench the bloody piece of wood from his chest because the atheist hero doesn't know how to pray. In hindsight it's a bit ridiculous, but to my wide-eyed ten year old self it was a stunning and unexpected highlight of the picture. In fact I'd go so far as to call it Hammer's Italian moment — it doesn't really make any sense at all, but it must have had audiences wide-eyed in disbelief and shock in cinemas in 1968. Out of all the Dracula films Hammer made, this was the most successful. Some think it was because of its female stars (I'm sure Hammer boss James Carreras did, and it was even retitled 'Dracula et les Femmes' in France). I like to think it was because of the film's many over the top moments. The first victim is found trussed up in a bell inside a church, with that lovely effect of blood running down the rope. No-one seems to question that Dracula hadn't actually been brought back to life yet. When he is, it's because of blood unconvincingly trickling all the way from a priest Ewan Hooper's gashed head into Dracula's mouth as he lies beneath some extremely thin ice on a mountain slope. A moment later and Dracula's up and about, reflected (Shock! Horror! Heresy!) in the icy mountain stream, and busy bending the fairly hopeless (and very dubbed) Ewan to his will. After this Dracula decides that, rather than vampirise the local female populace (who would all no doubt resemble 1960s busty British starlets on the make) he would rather get his revenge on the Monsignor (Rupert Davies) who has locked him out of his castle. If I was Dracula I'd have got Ewan to shift that cross and then gone looking for Jacqueline Pearce or Barbara Shelley (again), but instead we end up meeting beery Barry Andrews who's in love with blonde busty Veronica Carlson. Before you can say "Dracula's not actually in this very much, is he?" Mr Lee is hissing, acting menacing, and saying very little. But never mind, there's a fun chase across rooftops, via horse and carriage, and finally that climactic battle that results in Dracula getting flung off a cliff and onto the handily pre-positioned crucifix. Mr Lee thrashes around very effectively, thank you very much, before dissolving in a puddle of goo. Roll credits to James Bernard's theme in a major key for a change.

I must admit I've seen Dracula Has Risen From the Grave many times and writing this makes me want to watch it again. It doesn't make a lot of sense and it doesn't even feature Dracula that much, but it's Hammer Films at the company's pinnacle of success. Thrilling, gory, sexy, colourful, crazy, over the top, beautifully designed, gorgeously photographed and bombastically scored. Heaving bosoms, hissing Dracula and hysterically over the top at points, if you stopped people in the street when I was growing up and mentioned Hammer to them, this is what it meant.

BLOOD FROM THE MUMMY'S TOMB (1971)

While Hammer managed to do a number of interesting things with Dracula and Frankenstein, it wasn't until their fourth mummy picture that they managed to do something truly original with this particular classic movie monster. Shot in red brick environs in the middle of an early 1970s winter, can you think of any other successful mummy picture that has a contemporary setting? Good old Hammer. Only at the height of their powers could they take a minor Bram Stoker novel, fill it with slashed throats, a crawling severed hand (what exactly was the point of that, by the way?) and a sexy leading lady, and just by accident produce an original and satisfying spin on the mummy theme that still works over forty years on.

Valerie Leon is Margaret, daughter to Andrew Keir's Professor Fuchs, an egyptologist of distinctly dodgy inclination, who seems to have half a rebuilt tomb in the basement of his ordinary-looking suburban house, a whole load of Egyptian artefacts, and a number of colleagues who want nothing more to do with him after some escapade abroad many years ago, which culminated in their breaking into the tomb of Queen Tera (Leon again). Tera, by all accounts, was a pretty naughty piece of work (well, she was definitely pretty, and sadly we don't get to find out how naughty she was capable of being). What's far more worrying is that the professor seems to have some poorly researched and badly thought out plan that involves the life of his daughter and the supplanting of her existence by said evil queen on the occasion of her next birthday.

Even more dodgy but better organised Corbeck (James

THE HAMMER OF DR VALENTINE

Villiers) is keen to see Tera rise again for his own ends, and he aims to assist the queen in reclaiming the artifacts needed to complete the ceremony. George Coulouris is locked up in one of the best Hammer loony bins and, in a superbly edited and shot bit of mayhem, ends up dead and his snake statue gone. Hugh Burden has a heart attack and has his jackal skull stolen, and fortune teller Rosalie Crutchley gets her cat pinched while her companion (labelled 'Saturnine Man' in the credits) looks on. It's all for nothing of course as the surviving cast members succumb to another what-shall-we-do-to-end-it-oh-let's-have-the-roof-fall-in Hammer climax, with either Margaret or Tera ended up being mummified for real in a closing shot that's possibly the best one in a film that's really rather good all the way through.

With a title that means nothing other than that James Carreras had learned to copy Tony Tenser's approach to titling films by reaching into a box of cards labelled with 'horror' words until the right combination came up, a director who died before filming finished, a star who left once filming had started, and a script by a writer who was both banned from the set and notorious for screenplays that were a bit difficult to make any sense of sometimes, it's a wonder that Blood From the Mummy's Tomb is any good at all. What's more surprising than that is that it's actually well worth watching, and is easily the best (along with the 1959 The Mummy) of the films Hammer made that had a connection to ancient Egypt. It's rare that the fourth movie in any horror film cycle has anything to commend it, and following in the wake of Curse of the Mummy's Tomb and The Mummy's Shroud one could be forgiven for expecting Hammer's Mummy IV to be a right load of derivative old rubbish. Instead it's original, well directed, and being shot in what looks like the depths of winter

111

only serves to heighten the creepy atmosphere that pervades the movie right up to that classic final shot. That image scared me silly, by the way, when I watched this on its 'First Showing on British Television' (the Radio Times always told you if a movie was a premiere in those days) as the second half of a BBC2 double bill. Which if course is why it's here as the second of Dr Valentine's Hammer-inspired deaths.

The acting is fine throughout, with the usual collection of British character actors and eccentrics (Aubrey Morris take a bow you lovable weirdo, you) and Valerie Leon, having been used as decorative set dressing in a number of Carry Ons, getting the role that she was born to play. Hammer didn't always get their casting right but she is uncannily perfect for the roles of both Tera and Margaret. Fine stuff all round, Blood From the Mummy's Tomb is a Hammer film that's definitely worth preserving. A personal favourite.

FEAR IN THE NIGHT (1971)

I well remember watching this for the first time. I had just got out of hospital having suffered a particularly nasty case of appendicitis. The extent of the peritonitis I had suffered as a consequence of the organ's rupture was entirely my own fault. At the tender age of eleven I refused to be taken to hospital, and even pretended I was recovering from the appalling abdominal pain from which I had been suffering, solely so I could stay up to watch Peter Cushing star in Corruption (1967). Seeing as the film was never shown on television again and has not surfaced on DVD uncut until this year I have to stay I still feel justified in having watched Sir John

Rowan hack a prostitute's head off while I clutched at my own abdomen and wished that the awful pain in my right iliac fossa would go away.

But enough of my medical history. The next week I was back at home and sitting in the armchair, some heavy silk sutures holding my right sided gridiron incision together, as I settled down to watch the next in ATV's Peter Cushing season. Fear in the Night was the last gasp of the Hammer psycho thriller. I don't really count the pretty dire Straight On Till Morning, as that's a different kettle of fish altogether, one that I like to call dull, pretentious, and failed. Fear in the Night is the hoary old plot of trying to drive some poor young girl mad and get her to think events are not at all as they seem. Pretty Judy Geeson marries Ralph Bates and goes to live with him at an isolated public school run by Michael Carmichael and his prosthetic arm (Cushing in tiny spectacles) and his wife Molly and her twelve bore shotgun (Joan Collins doing her usual black widow routine even though her husband is still alive — for the moment anyway). The school is entirely bereft of pupils but the empty classrooms have tape recordings installed so mad Mr Carmichael can relive the glory days of when he was still allowed near children.

The Hammer of Dr Valentine was originally going to open with someone being chased down empty school corridors while children's voices screamed at them through loudspeakers. I liked the idea so much I thought it deserved more space than I was intending the opening chapter to have. So it got pushed further into the book and also allowed me to have a lot of fun trying to remember all those noun declensions and verb conjugations from my own school classics lessons.

SHE (1965)

I didn't want every death in the book to be from a Hammer Dracula, Frankenstein or Mummy picture. Similarly I didn't want to include too many obscure films that people might not know about. Having someone chased by stop-motion dinosaurs and girls in fur bikinis was an appealing prospect, but the book wasn't going to be called The Hammer Acid Trip of Dr Valentine, so I reigned in any ambitions for some more bizarre Hammer homages. Besides, at this point I was still contemplating a Slave Girls chapter, where someone was going to get skewered on a giant white rhino horn while a room full of Martine Beswick and Edina Ronay lookalikes swayed and gyrated while wearing very little. Sometimes people ask me why I write and I hope that's helped provide an answer.

Anyway, having dispensed with a room full of Edinas, I thought epic Hammer would do very nicely. Plus, the climactic scene of She, where Ursula Andress turns into an old hag and then falls to bits before a horrified John Richardson's eyes, was one of my first memories of being terrified to the point of running out of my parents' lounge. I think it must have been a Saturday afternoon BBC2 screening, and I must have been about five. Lots of horror writers have fears about peculiar things. One of mine is old ladies, for reasons I won't go into too much here, but I'm sure She didn't help things.

So I had to have a lady dissolve, because for me that's the whole essence of the film. The rest was working out how to do it. I also hope that this chapter, with Dr Valentine as a cosmetics expert, will hopefully have those familiar with the first volume thinking nostalgically of Vincent Price's turn as 'Butch' in my favourite film of all time, Theatre of Blood. Hammer buffs will already have worked out where 'Dr Chantler Day' is from, and a quick check of the film's credits will explain it to anyone else who wants to know.

PARANOIAC! (1965)

This one's only mentioned in passing (along with 1963's Phantom of the Opera). I wanted a reference to it because it's my very favourite of the black and white Hammer psycho-thrillers that tended to play as B-features to their more colourful A pictures. A lot of people prefer Susan Strasberg in Scream of Fear (1961) but I'll take mad old Oliver Reed chatting to his rotting brother as he plays the organ anytime. Another one from BBC2 double bill days, I now own this on a sparkling Blu-ray and wonder, like I do with so many films, how on earth I watched this one in pan and scan. Freddie Francis' direction is often creative and never dull, there's a nice creepy score from Elizabeth Lutyens (daughter of Sir Edwin), and Janette Scott makes for a pretty put-upon heroine. I've got Dr Valentine playing Bach's Prelude in E Minor because that's one of the first pieces I learned when I started playing the church organ. Sadly, I don't have one in my house. I don't have a terrified Daily Mail reporter tied to a chair, either, I promise. Would I lie to you?

HANDS OF THE RIPPER (1971)

Now, here we have another favourite of mine. Hands of the Ripper is a fascinating, gorgeous, and superbly made mixture of tragic love story and (for its time, certainly) gory slasher picture. I first watched it during one Christmas in the early 1980s (the BBC were good to us back then), came upstairs and related the entire plot to my ten year old younger brother who was still awake at well past one in the morning, and since then I've revisited it regularly. It's another Hammer that I could wax lyrical about for ages because I love pretty much everything about it. Eric Porter is splendid as the movie's 'mad scientist' where in this case the science is psychology rather than surgery or any 'physical' discipline. Angharad Rees is tiny, delicate, and yet somehow believable as both the helpless Anna and the spirit of Jack the Ripper. In fact it's impossible to believe that any other actress could have done a better job. Christopher Gunning's music plays up to the film's emotional core and this could quite possibly be director Peter Sasdy's best film. All this and Dora Bryan getting skewered with a poker when we're barely past the credits — what more could you want?

THE REPTILE (1966)

Another one I had to include and, after Fear in the Night, the second 'creative death' I came up with for the book. What better Hammer film to suit a fairground ride? Originally it was to be a roller-coaster but I felt the practicalities of being able to construct such a thing were beyond the bounds of even Dr Valentine's capabilities. (Although one of my favourite moments in the non-Hammer Dr Phibes Rises Again is when someone says they wouldn't be surprised if Phibes had created the storm they are currently experiencing. Quite where he gets a giant fan from in the desert is one of those marvellous movie moments that is simply Not To Be Questioned).

Back to The Reptile. This is a Hammer it took me a long while to catch up with (the Studio Canal Blu-ray is a treat, by the way) but the still of Jacqueline Pearce in her Roy Ashton snake mask had been a familiar feature of horror film books ever since I started reading them. I remember being delighted when, at age ten, we had a school trip to Newport to view an art exhibition about masks. It was there as part of the display. I gave a short summary to the rest of the class about what I knew of the film, much to my form teacher's surprise.

The Reptile is a fairly minor Hammer film, but I think there's a lot to commend it. Miss Pearce is splendidly sensuous in her slinky green dress, and the bit where she has a little bit of dialogue while in her snake form is actually oddly sexy — shades of what movies like Robert Siodmak's The Cobra Woman (1944) promised on the posters but never delivered. The colour photography is lush and Don Banks delivers music that's subtler and more varied than James Bernard's work for the company.

Dr Terror's Haunted Cornish Funfair also features references to a number of other Cornish horror films, including Hammer's own Plague of the Zombies (1966), Sidney J Furie's Dr Blood's Coffin (1961) and Tom Parkinson and Ted Hooker's 1971 Mike Raven-starrer Crucible of Terror, where Me Me Lay gets coated in bronze.

On a note that's probably not at all interesting to anyone, this chapter also features a cameo appearance by my car. It's given me years of faithful service and so I thought it deserved a mention. I wonder if this is a first. There's also a cameo by my wife's voodoo doll. If that's not a first I'd like to read the book that did that one before me.

FRANKENSTEIN MUST BE DESTROYED (1969)

Here's another favourite of mine, and one I first saw under unusual conditions. Back in the old days (i.e. the late 1970s) HTV Cymru was the Welsh regional broadcaster on behalf of Independent Television, or ITV, which is now vastly more homogenised and dull in its programming than it was back then. Or at least that's how it feels. Anyway, it was not unusual for HTV Cymru to broadcast popular movies dubbed into Welsh. Seeing as neither I nor my family spoke the language, this often led to some confused but nevertheless amusing evenings. I well remember watching George Stevens' classic Western Shane (1953) with my dad as we tried to work out what Alan Ladd was actually talking about, speaking as he was in Welsh with a strong Blaenavon accent.

I kept my fingers crossed that a Tuesday night showing of Hammer's Frankenstein Must Be Destroyed was not going to suffer the same indignity, but sadly it was not to be. The hand-drawn title card 'Rhaid Distro Frankenstein' should have warned me, of course (I think that's what it said) but bear in mind that the first few scenes of the film feature no dialogue at all. By the time we got to Thorley Walters interrogating Harold Goodwin, both of them sounding as if they came from the far side of Merthyr Tydfil, I was so involved with the film that it was difficult to tear myself away. And hearing Peter Cushing speak in Welsh was, I am sure you will appreciate, a quite singular experience.

It was only many years later that I got to see Frankenstein Must Be Destroyed in English, but even now I can remember my ten year old self staring at that Welsh version, wishing desperately that I could understand what on earth was going on. Who knows?

Perhaps that's why I developed such an affection for the more surreal and dubbed Euro-Horrors of the 1970s later in life.

I haven't talked about the film at all, and I apologise for that, but I'm sure you'll understand that's something I've wanted to get off my chest for many, many years. Frankenstein Must Be Destroyed is a cracking piece of Hammer horror. Peter Cushing's Baron Frankenstein had, by this time, become ruthless, amoral, and a complete and utter bastard. Of all of his performances as Frankenstein, this is my favourite, and I can watch him endlessly in it. Never mind soppy Simon Ward and busty Veronica Carlson, bastard Peter Cushing is the reason I love this film, whether he's sawing open a skull to get at the facts the poor chap's brain holds, or being deliciously pretend-sympathetic to Maxine Audley when she comes to unexpectedly visit. Everyone complains about the rape scene (put in at James Carreras' insistence) and it doesn't need to be there, but it does make us think Frankenstein's even more of a bastard than we do already.

Originally I planned to have the climax from Frankenstein Be Destroyed be mirrored as the climax of Hammer of Dr Valentine, but when I came to write it I realised the story couldn't end there. And so we come to...

ALL THE OTHERS...

I wanted to try and include references to as many Hammer films as possible. When the epiphany struck that the climax had to take place at Oakley Court, I thought it was about time the police sat down with a crate of DVDs and worked their way through some old favourites. Slave Girls (1968) finally gets a mention (if you haven't seen it, by the way, it's really not that great. My great friend and fellow movie enthusiast Guy Adams called it "invariably the last movie in your Ultimate Hammer Collection to draw attention. It rattles at the bottom like a semi-crushed Orange Cream in the Christmas Chocolate Tin." I rather like Orange Cream, but I don't think I need to watch Slave Girls again in a hurry. The Viking Queen (1967) is another one that probably won't get screened again soon, along with The Pirates of Blood River (1962). Hammer managed a nice line in kids' adventure pictures for the Saturday morning crowd (so Mum and Dad could go shopping or recover from hangovers from the night before) but I must confess I find them mainly curios now.

Legend of the Seven Golden Vampires (1974), however, is a picture I love. Made just after the blink-and-you'll-miss-it early 1970s craze for martial arts movies reached its peak, it's a crazy melange of East meets West, with Dracula in pantomime greasepaint, rotting vampires where you can tell the make-up is a mask even from quite a long way away, loads of chop-socky action, Julie Ege's chest wobbling about a bit in a vest, Peter Cushing holding it all together, and one of James Bernard's best scores. The whole sequence near the beginning where the dead rise from their graves to create a weird zombie army is an all-time classic bit of Hammer.

Captain Clegg, or Night Creatures (1961) is another Saturday morning pic that I must confess a sneaking liking for, probably because it has Cushing, Oliver Reed, Patrick Allen and Yvonne Romain, all of whom add colour to the swashbuckling adventure. Oh, and dear old Milton Reid, tied to a post after having his ears cut off in an opening scene that misleads us into thinking this is going to be a gorier pirate adventure than it actually is.

Sorry Straight On Till Morning (1972), but I never really liked you, so you get it in the neck from both Dr Valentine and DCI Longdon at the end here. Nightmare (1964) is the Hammer psycho-thriller where I finally wondered how audiences of the time could believe it was possible to produce an accurate, realistic, life-like mask of someone that could fit perfectly over someone else's face and, in some cases, alter their body shape and language so they looked exactly like the person they were impersonating. So here's my little homage to that particular bit of 1960s implausibility.

And then we have a net drop from the ceiling, just like in Curse of the Mummy's Tomb (1964) — I said I wanted to pack in as many references as possible. For the record, I consider this to be Hammer's worst mummy picture. I much prefer The Mummy's Shroud (1967) which exhibits a cruelty and creativity to its murders (and especially in the way they're filmed) that elevates it a bit above Michael Carreras' pedestrian effort. Dickie Owen's mummy appearing at the top of a flight of fog-shrouded stone steps is almost worth the price of admission, though.

For the climax, I pondered for all of a microsecond if it might be too cliched to pay homage to Dracula (1958), and then I remembered what kind of a book this was meant to be and wondered how on earth I could have considered leaving it out. Hammer's version of Stoker's novel is one of my favourite remakes of all time. It's a great film for so many reasons — performance, photography and music being just a few, but the reasons I think it's one of the greatest are twofold. First, until it came out (Curse of Frankenstein being a bit of a warm-up act) horror as a film genre was all but dead, considered to be black and white kiddie matinee monster fare but certainly not something worthy of adult attention. Then along came Dracula, with its vivid, marvellous colour, its blood and gore and pretty girls with heaving bosoms. The film single-handedly changed the face of the horror film forever — and in so many good ways. It also showed that sometimes British really was best, and gave us a chance to shine in the international market at something we could be really good at — quality, atmospheric well-made horror. Stop people in the street today and they can still tell you what Hammer Horror is because it really was that momentous a sea change. Second, Dracula really is the way to approach a remake — it doesn't slavishly copy the original, or the book on which it's based — instead it swirled its satin-lined cape, bared its fangs and did its own outrageous thing in the context of the social and cultural climate of the time. It was one of the first horror films I ever saw and I still consider myself very lucky to have encountered the good stuff so early on. So here's that splendid climax once more, this time à la Dr Valentine, complete with curtain-pulling-down scene.

And we're still not finished! Once he's been chased across the rooftops of Oakley Court (someone has to put that in a film sometime) Valentine references, in order, the climaxes of Don Sharp's Kiss of the Vampire (1963), Terence Fisher's Brides of Dracula (1960) and To the Devil Daughter (1976) — Hammer's last horror film until things started up again recently, and possibly the worst climax to a Hammer horror ever.

Finally, Valentine's escape. I'll confess that right up until the last page I wasn't sure if he was going to get away this time or not, but the idea of a funeral cortege on the Thames was too good not to use, even it if felt more Phibes than Hammer. It's neither, of course. The message Valentine leaves Longdon reveals what film is being referenced here, and it's nothing to do with Hammer at all.

Because in the next book, Dr Valentine will be...

...oh, I'll leave that for next time, shall I?

Yes indeed ladies and gentlemen, provided that The Hammer of Dr Valentine is favourably received, I can assure you that the good (bad?) doctor will be back, larger than life as ever, and with a whole new collection of creative murder methods for those he deems deserving of them in the third volume. All will be revealed in due course.

Until then, take care of yourselves, be nice to each other, and I (and Dr Valentine) will see you all again soon.

.

SNOWBOOKS HORROR NOVELLAS

THE BUREAU OF THEM

Cate Gardner

You're not the first to talk to your dead here, the vagrant said. The living always chase after their dead until they come upon their own.

Formed from shadow and dust, ghosts inhabit the abandoned office building, angry at the world that denies them. When Katy sees her deceased boyfriend in the window of the derelict building, she finds a way in, hoping to be reunited. Instead, the dead ignore, the dead do not see and only the monster that is Yarker Ryland has need of her there.

SCOURGE

Gary Fry

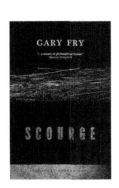

Felachnids: a race of mythical creatures that are rumoured to live in the dark Yorkshire countryside.

The yellow eyes, the double-jointed limbs, the heads that turned backwards whenever that was necessary. These creatures, which otherwise resembled humans, appeared to occupy a small village in North Yorkshire called Nathen.

And Lee Parker is determined to track them down.

SNOWBOOKS HORROR NOVELLAS

WITHIN THE WIND,
BENEATH THE SNOW

Ray Cluley

Gjerta knew there were darkteeth in the woods. They lived amongst the trees and in the shadows between them. And they were always there. Hidden. Quietly waiting.

Out of sight, but always in her mind...

www.snowbooks.com

Lightning Source UK Ltd.
Milton Keynes UK
UKOW05f1501160916

283153UK00009B/158/P